A Hole in My Heart

A Hole in
My Heart

Rie Charles

DUNDURN
TORONTO

Editor: Carrie Gleason
Design: Courtney Horner
Printer: Webcom
Cover design by Laura Boyle
Heart © shutterstock/art_of_sun
Life buoy © iStock/kutaytanir

Library and Archives Canada Cataloguing in Publication

Charles, Rie, 1946-, author
        A hole in my heart / Rie Charles.

Issued in print and electronic formats.
ISBN 978-1-4597-1052-8

        I. Title.

PS8605.H36917H65 2014   jC813'.6   C2013-908355-3
                                             C2013-908356-1

1   2   3   4   5   18   17   16   15   14

  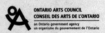

Conseil des Arts du Canada   Canada Council for the Arts   Canada   ONTARIO ARTS COUNCIL CONSEIL DES ARTS DE L'ONTARIO an Ontario government agency un organisme du gouvernement de l'Ontario

We acknowledge the support of the **Canada Council for the Arts** and the **Ontario Arts Council** for our publishing program. We also acknowledge the financial support of the **Government of Canada** through the **Canada Book Fund** and **Livres Canada Books**, and the **Government of Ontario** through the **Ontario Book Publishing Tax Credit** and the **Ontario Media Development Corporation**.

Care has been taken to trace the ownership of copyright material used in this book. The author and the publisher welcome any information enabling them to rectify any references or credits in subsequent editions.

                                            J. Kirk Howard, President

Printed and bound in Canada.

The publisher is not responsible for websites or their content unless they are owned by the publisher.

VISIT US AT
Dundurn.com | @dundurnpress | Facebook.com/dundurnpress | Pinterest.com/dundurnpress

Dundurn
3 Church Street, Suite 500
Toronto, Ontario, Canada
M5E 1M2

Gazelle Book Services Limited
White Cross Mills
High Town, Lancaster, England
LA1 4XS

Dundurn
2250 Military Road
Tonawanda, NY
U.S.A. 14150

for Bette

Author's Note

The characters in this book are all fictional, with one exception. I refer briefly to a doctor named Robertson. Doctor Ross Robertson was indeed a surgical pioneer in cardiology in Vancouver. For a brief article on the history of heart surgery in Vancouver with reference to Dr. Robertson, see Lawrence Burr, "Some early history of cardiac surgery in British Columbia," *Surgical Times (the newsletter of the UBC Department of Surgery)*, Winter 2007.

1

Staring out my bedroom window, I can't see beyond the waves of rain caught in the orange light of the streetlamp. I thought moving from Penticton to North Vancouver would make it better. But it's worse. Way worse. When it's not pouring, it's raining. When it's not raining, it's drizzling. My stupid skirts always smell of wet wool. If I wasn't already sodden and depressed, I'd get sodden and depressed just smelling them. And looking outside.

I want to go home.

I want things the way they used to be.

The front door bangs open. Thuds and stomps of feet.

"Hey, Bummer." It's my sister Dorothy. "How come your shoes were outside under the bushes?"

"Don't call me that, or I won't answer." My two sisters have blown in with suitcases and half the wet leaves of the neighbourhood. Plus my saddle shoes.

"Well, you just did. So how come?" Dorothy's holding my black and white leather shoes, muddy and wet, like they're two dead fish.

"Oh, bug off."

Dorothy is nineteen, blonde, and showy, and mainly can't talk about anything except clothes and boys. She's called Dot for short, but I call her Dotty in my head — usually — because that's what she's like. Dotty, as in crazy.

My other sister, Jan, who's the opposite of Dot, quiet and dark-haired, greets me with a hug, a "Hi, kiddli-winks," and a bundle of mail. I missed picking up the letters because I came in the house by the back door. I search through and pull one out.

"Oh good. It's from Lizzie," I say, and start up the stairs.

Dad emerges from his study in the basement where he always has his nose in a book or two or three. He grabs me by the shoulder. "Oh no you don't, girly. No disappearing into your room with that letter. You have to help with supper. And what's this ruining your shoes business?" I curse inwardly. "Go stuff some newspaper into them, put them by the hot air vent, and be back upstairs to help your sisters with supper. Lickety-split."

I yank up the bottom edge of my old sweater and shove it out in front of me. "Here." Dorothy, her pink-lip-sticked mouth screwed into an upside down *u*, drops one shoe at a time onto my waiting sweater-tray. "How are you going to be a nurse if you don't even like dirty shoes? What about wiping up sick?" I steal a glance at Jan. She smirks. "And wiping old men's you-know-whatsits?"

"Yeah, well, at least I'll get to give needles and can practise by sticking them into you."

"Stop that bickering. Get a move on, all of you." Dad's voice is harsh. He's more than irritated. "I'm hungry. We need to get supper started." Somehow he's only around when I don't want him to be. "Nora, did you pick the carrots?"

I shake my head, no. Now it's Dorothy's turn to smirk.

During the weekdays, both Janet and Dorothy live in the student nurses' residence at St. Paul's Hospital in Vancouver. They only come home on the weekends. Last year, after grade twelve, Dorothy didn't want to do thirteen so she worked in the office of a local motel for half the year and twiddled her thumbs the rest. But Mum and Dad said she had to have further education. The rest of us have to, too. I don't know why Dot, though, because all she ever wants to do is go out with boys. Anyway, when Jan applied to St. Paul's, so did Dorothy. Me, on the other hand, I'm stuck in North Vancouver going to Sutherland Junior High.

I want a new life. Or, better still, my old one back.

I can hear my silly sisters upstairs laughing and giggling. They come home so full of themselves. I scrunch up a double page of yesterday's Vancouver *Province* and wedge it into the toe of my right shoe. There's Dot carrying on — "*Oooh*, isn't Dr. Wispinski gorgeous? And Dr. Graydon? *Aaahh*, would I love to go out with him." What a bunch of malarkey.

Last Saturday night, just to be mean, I locked the basement door so that when Jan and Dorothy came home, they had to come in the kitchen entrance and say good night to their dates under the bright outside light. Dot kissed a guy called Jerry McGibbon in full view of the neighbourhood. His Brylcreemed hair curled over his forehead like a horn. Dot thinks he's so cool. Drool, cool, my eye. *How come, Mum, you have three dumb daughters?*

I jam more scrunched-up newspaper into the shoes. It feels good — like punching or pounding. My anger jams down and scrunches up too. I drop my shoes onto the heating duct. Maybe, like Mum, I'll get out of this life entirely.

"Hurry up, Bummer," Dorothy calls down the stairs. "Where're the carrots?"

I step wide around the girls' suitcases on the landing, climb the remaining stairs two at a time, and burst into the kitchen. "In the garden, where they belong."

"Quit sassing me, you little brat." Dorothy grates potatoes into a bowl. "Dad says you're to pick the carrots, so go pick. And Jan, would you *pulleeease*" — emphasizing and stretching the word out as only Dot can do — "put away our suitcases or you-know-who will ruin them?"

How come she gets a please and I don't?

Mean old witch.

• • •

"Here." I toss a handful of muddy, scraggly carrots into the sink. Their green tails splat bits of black on the counter.

"Hey, watch it. You're getting dirt in the potatoes. You should've rinsed them outside."

"And here's some more dirt." I fling my socks at Dorothy, the ones I'd tramped around outside in after I kicked off my shoes. She ducks.

"You drip. Dad," her voices rises, "tell Nora to do something right." Dorothy jams her hair behind her ears.

"Whine to Daddy, eh?"

Dorothy's face flushes.

"Oh, go do something useful — like put the sausages on."

"Why can't Janet?"

"Just go do it." Jan is nowhere to be seen when Dot and I argue. "And while you're at it, change that sweater. It's filthy."

"You're not my mother, so shut up."

Silence.

Dad enters the kitchen. Of course. He's always there when I do something mean, never when Dorothy does. His voice is low and cold. "You apologize to your sister and don't use those words in this house again. Ever." More silence. I'm trying to think of something not smart-alecky but I'm definitely having trouble with basic thinking. "Well?"

"The you're-not-my-mother part or the shut-up part?" Dad's normally reddish face — from his freckles that cover almost everything — deepens to explosive red. His ears seem to stick out further too. This is a clear sign of a soon-to-happen blowup. Backtalking is not allowed.

"Sorry, Dad. Yes, Dad." I turn to my sister and put on the sweetest, smarmiest smile so she knows I don't mean it. But Dad can't see. "Sorry, Dotty." The room relaxes. Somewhat. I yank the cast-iron frying pan from under the stove, bang it down on the right back element, and plop the sausages on.

"Don't forget to prick them."

I hunch my shoulders, force them down with a sigh. Then, with vicious delight, I spear each sausage once, twice, three times. There are words I want to say but don't. Even in my head. I pat the letter in my pocket and watch the sausages sizzle and spit.

• • •

Penticton
September 6, 1959

Dear Nora,
I miss you. Jenny's still away and I have no one to talk to at school.

It must be a lot better going to a junior high than a straight high school. The big kids aren't so big and you don't have to wait for five or six years to be at the top of the totem pole like here at Pen High. Have you seen any totem poles yet, for real?

So far Mrs. Cramer is nice. I sit smack in the middle of the middle row in homeroom. She put us in alphabetical order, so Jenny will be right up at the front of the class near the window when she comes back. Vicki sits one over from me but she seems really cozy with a new girl with a fancy name — Melinda, the teacher called her, but, I thinks she wants to be called Linda. She wears frilly blouses with a sweater half open in front. She says it's the latest 1959 fashion in Winnipeg, where she comes from.

Who are your new friends? Your letter sounded a bit lonesome. I thought you were really looking forward to moving, getting away from here. The school is having a Halloween party. The grade twelves and the student council are putting it on. I don't I want to go because I'll have to sit on the sidelines. But I probably will because Jenny will insist.

I had to go to the doctor's again. You'd think I'd be used to it after all these years. I hate having to undress in front of him. I hate him putting his stethoscope all over my chest and back. My parents use the term blue baby for my condition but he says Tetralogy of Fallot, the fancy medical term which means the same thing, but just makes me feel sicker. Much worse than I think I am. My purple toes and lips and fingernails are just my purple toes and lips and fingernails. Nobody else's. They're me — but they do remind me of my breathing difficulties, my tiredness, a sign of what's wrong inside.

Apparently the doctor I see in Vancouver has been doing a new type of surgery for kids like me. That means going into hospital again sometime in the next few months, another operation, and another big scar on my chest, I guess. That I am not looking forward to, the hospital, the operation, or the scar. But I'll get to see you so that's good. And get fixed.

My little brothers are bugging me. What's new? They're trying to snatch the paper from me as I write. They want me to quiz them from *World Book* again. I have to go before they rip this.

Please write often.

Your cousin,
Lizzie

PS I got *Anne of the Island* out of the library. Have you read it?

2

I figure I'd got through the shoe business without too much bother but Janet comes into my room the next evening, just before supper, peeling off her apron. I know something's up. "Shove over." She squeezes in beside me on the bed. "So how come your shoes were outside in the bushes?"

I know I'll cry if I tell her. No one cries in my family except me, and I know I'm not supposed to. It's not the crying I mind, actually, but the wet and wilted feeling afterward. No strength. Nothing inside. Like a slobbery, squished balloon. Why is it just me who cries?

Pushing myself up sideways on my left elbow, I crank up the corners of my mouth to meet my cheeks and reply to Jan with my own question. "What happened at nursing school this week? Anything neat?"

"Yeah, we got to make beds." She grins and seems to forget she asked me a question.

"You call making beds neat?"

"The class is called 'Nursing Arts.' We practise doing stuff we'll have to do on wards."

"But you've made your own bed since you were little. What's the point?"

"Not the way they want them — with special tight corners and pulling the bottom sheet so hard your fingers almost break. Plus, we have to make the bed with someone in it." She grabs the blankets and gives them a yank like she's straightening my covers. I topple onto my back.

"Hey, stop that." I laugh a little bit.

"Miss Mackie, our nursing instructor, pulls the bed apart if the corners aren't just right. Then we have to start all over again." She grimaces. "My bed was fine except I forgot to put the folded-in end of the pillowcase away from the door. Imagine. There's even a right direction for pillows." Jan tosses her balled-up apron at me. It unravels into long arms of cloth.

"Did she make you do it again?"

"No, thank heavens. But don't tell, okay?

"Don't tell what?"

"When you've promised not to say anything, I'll tell you." Even though I hate promising like that, this seems pretty safe.

"I promise." I cross my heart.

"Dot had to do hers twice over." Now we both laugh, for real. I pitch the apron back at Jan. She crams it down my shirt. And then, right when I think we're far away from my shoes and school and me, she says, "So how come your shoes were outside?"

I focus on her hair, as if I haven't heard. "How do you like your new hairdo?" She got it cut really short to start nursing.

"Easy to look after and great for when we get our nursing caps." She sweeps her hands along the sides of her hair towards the ducktail at the back. In my opinion, she looks like a girl version of Elvis Presley. "I couldn't fiddle with it and put it up every day the way Dot does." She pokes me in the stomach. "You can't avoid answering forever. How come your shoes were outside?"

I take a deep breath. "I hate it here. No one likes me." Darn. I feel the tears rising.

"You've been at school one week. That's all. Liking a new place takes time."

"But we've been in North Vancouver three weeks and you like nursing already, don't you?"

"Yeah, but that's different. I'm there with a purpose — to learn to be a nurse. The others all want to be nurses too. High school's different."

"Not that different."

She can't drop it. "Did something bad happen on Friday?"

"My shoes." I squinch up my eyes, forcing the tears back. "And not just then. They tease me about them all the time. That's why I kicked them into the chrysanthemums."

"Your shoes? I thought you loved those shoes. I remember you and Mum getting them last spring."

Why does she have to remind me? As if I can forget. Mum and I went shopping together at that shoe store on Main Street. Mum told a corny elephant joke. Something about "How do you tell an elephant from an egg?" I hooted with laughter when she replied in a pretend snotty sort of voice, "Well, I'm not going to send you out for a dozen eggs." She was all rosy and happy then.

"A lot of the girls in Penticton wear oxfords and saddle shoes. At least they did last spring. Here they wear dainty slingbacks, pretty shoes made of patent leather, or penny loafers, not big, ugly, clumpy oxfords. And my shoes always look extra crappy because I get smudges of white polish all over the black patches. I told Dad but he says I can't have new ones. I have to wear sensible shoes, not even penny loafers. No one here wears sensible shoes." My tear squinching fails. I'm full-blown crying. I shift my cheek away from the wet-smeared patch on my pillowcase. "I don't like being laughed at. They even tease me about my clothes. I want to go back to Penticton. I want things the way they were."

"Oh kiddliwinks. We all do. But Mum's not coming back. Just try to be happy. Try to look on the bright side."

"Oh, you sound like Dad. Or old Mrs. Garnett. She patted me on the head at Mum's funeral and said, 'Things will be fine, dear. Your mother would want you to be happy.' Well, I'm not happy. And I'll never be happy again. Nothing's ever going to be the same."

"I didn't say things were ever going to be the same." Jan strokes my back. "It's not the same for me either."

"Yeah, but you chose to leave Penticton. I didn't." I flip over. "Oh, Jan, don't adults realize things are never going to be happy or nice or wonderful? When Mrs. Garnett said that with her gushy smile, I just wanted Mum to sit up in her coffin and tell her to go jump in the lake. That would have scared the pants off her."

I can see Jan trying not to smile, but she does. I sort of do too.

"It's not fair. You and Dot had Mum much longer than I did. Besides, you have each other. I have nobody."

"What do you mean *nobody?* You've got Dad."

"No I don't. He's always in his office or behind a newspaper or staring out the window." I groan into my pillow. "If I had nice shoes at least, I'd have friends." Jan takes a big breath, then lets it out long and slowly like a sigh.

"Mum always used to say if kids tease you they like you, they want your attention."

"Yeah, when were you ever teased at school?"

"You have to ignore them, try not to react. Make some smart-aleck comment like, *You're just jealous. Don't know style when you see it.* Something like that."

"Sure, Jan." My blackboard glowers down at us.

> Why did you want to leave me, Mum?
> Why did you have to die?
> I want you back

"And by the way, Mum didn't want to die, Nor. She got sick and Dad couldn't save her. What do you think it was like for her, having to leave her lovely youngest daughter who is only twelve years old?"

I jump off the bed, rub out the chalk words and replace them with:

> I will never be happy and have friends
> here if I have to wear saddle shoes.
> So there!!!

• • •

It's Sunday. I'm on my bed as usual. Janet and Dot have gone back to St. Paul's. I stare at the ceiling or off into

21

space, with Lizzie's letter on my chest, arms curled under my head. A spider crawls along the crinkly crack that runs towards the window. It's not fair. Vicki Matthews is my best friend. Or was. I wrote but she hasn't written back. I even asked her to come for a visit. Now she has another best friend. I don't. And here everybody's snooty. So I'm snooty back.

3

I wander along the hall after Art class the next afternoon, daydreaming as usual. I'm no good at art but the project we have right now is cool. We wax-crayon a sheet of paper in crazy shapes of red, green, pink, yellow, or whatever, then go over it with another thick layer of black. With something not too sharp — I'm using an old letter opener from home — we scratch a design in the black to reveal the colours below. I planned a garden scene with trees, flowers, tools, and a wheelbarrow. But when I actually drew it out on the paper, the tools were too big and the flowers in the wrong place. So the flowers turned out green and the wheelbarrow looked like an octopus with two arms. What do you call a two-armed octopus? A diptopus?

But I still liked the project.

Anyway, so there I am sauntering down the hallway to Math, trying to figure out in my head how to redraw it, when *whammo*. Someone sticks out a foot and I'm on the floor along with my books. I reach out to stop my fall. My hands catch at a boy's pants. "Hey, what the ..." The guy grabs at his trousers and other kids start laughing.

I duck into the girls' washroom right around the corner. I can feel my face burning. I'm breathing fast. Why is it always me? I hear catcalls from behind. "Hey, she likes you, Gord. Trying to pull your pants down. Ha. Ha. What about her pants, Gord?"

Funn-eee. Hardi har har, I say to myself.

The next thing I hear is a whoop, a glug, and a slop, from inside the washroom. More wretching and throw-up sounds. Out of one of the stalls comes a girl in my Science class, her face wet and green. She glares.

"Don't you breathe a word." I hand her some paper towels. She has wisps of hair plastered to the sides of her cheeks, one curl on either side. Her kiss curls and black hair remind me of Debbie Charlton back in Penticton. We weren't friends but she was popular, especially with certain guys. Her glare turns to a scowl. "I said, don't you breathe a word."

"Why would I?" I reply. In my head I think, *Who would I tell anyway?* Actually, I'm still too shaken by my fall to think. I skedaddle to Math class.

• • •

My lockers are on the bottom floor of the north wing of the school, three down from the green double doors to outside. As I exit after school, a voice calls out. There are two girls slouched on the low cement wall, cigarettes dangling from their hands.

"You're new here, eh?" It's the girl from the washroom. "What's your name?" She has that same eye fluttery sort of way Debbie has too. "I'm Dolores and this here's my friend Trudy."

"I'm Nora. Aren't you in my Science class?" Dolores wears a tight mauve sweater set and matching purple skirt. Trudy too, only her sweater and skirt are blue. I assume Dolores is going to mention the up-chucking. But no.

"Wanna smoke?" I hesitate for a moment. My dad doesn't approve of smoking, especially for girls. He says it makes them look cheap. I sort of agree.

"Sure. Why not?" I blurt out. I squeeze the lit cigarette between my index and middle fingers and take a puff. It takes all my concentration not to cough or choke, and to will my mouth and eyes to look calm. I imagine myself a glamorous movie star like Kim Novak, in the poster my sister Dot has on her wall, dancing and smoking with Frank Sinatra. It doesn't help. The air in my throat burns. I cough and sputter.

"See, I told you she wouldn't know how to inhale." Trudy laughs a sharp, piercing laugh. Dolores takes one last drag on her cigarette and tosses it at my feet.

"Who got you those? Your grandma?" She smirks and stomps out the cigarette. The two of them are off.

My shoes again.

Of course I don't answer back with something clever. Her words go inside and sit like lumpy porridge. And I hate porridge — even without lumps.

• • •

It's 5:15 now and I rattle around in the kitchen making supper — spaghetti again. I fry up some onions and ground beef, add sauce from a can, and let it simmer while I boil the water for the pasta. I set the table for two, with a container of grated Parmesan cheese in the middle, the tea pot ready for Dad's tea, and a plate of cookies for dessert.

By six, I'm starving and I go ahead and eat, even though Dad's not home from the hospital. In Penticton he was a family doctor but now he's learning to be a surgeon at the Vancouver General. That's why we moved to the Coast. Or part of the reason. I open my library book to read as I slurp up the mound of spaghetti. The meal doesn't take long to finish, so I read a bit more, sipping on my milk and ignoring the call of the cookies. I decide to leave them to share with Dad later. Eventually, I dump my dirty dishes and cutlery into the sink and run the water for washing up.

I startle as the door opens. Dad drops his briefcase on the floor, shrugs his coat into the hall closet, and heads up the stairs towards me in the kitchen.

"I couldn't get away earlier," he mumbles as he upturns the cold glob of cooked spaghetti pasta into a large bowl, dumps the remaining lukewarm sauce over it, and heads back down the stairs to his office.

"Aren't you going to eat with me?" I call out.

"You've eaten."

"I was going to have my dessert with you…." But he's already disappeared into the basement.

I add soap to the dishwater and plunge in my hands. First my milk glass, then my plate, spoon and fork, the cutting board and knives. One after the other I scrub them, harder than usual. *Why do I always have to do everything?* One after the other I rinse each item under the tap. *Why won't he eat with me?* I can feel my breathing get faster. *And can't he even say hello?* I grab the large pasta pot lined with the goo of cooked spaghetti, lift it to shoulder height, and smash it down into the water. Gobs of greasy pink water splatter all over — on my apron, the cupboards, the countertop, the surrounding clean dishes, and even on the floor. I ball up my apron, fling it to the floor and stomp out, yelling, "I hate it here, absolutely hate it here. And you don't care one little bit."

I slam the door to my bedroom behind me.

I bury, or pretend to bury, my head in my Math homework. In my scribbler I draw a careful line with a ruler beneath the last question the way we're supposed to. But my hands are shaky like the rest of me and I have to rub it out twice before I get it right. I start on number fourteen. I really don't mind Math. Not because it's fascinating or dead easy, but because, unlike in Penticton, Mr. Keen doesn't make us work on the blackboard or answer questions in front of the class. He says virtually the same thing every day, changing the numbers of course. "Read page thirty-two and do questions two to seventeen in your scribbler."

Anyway, there I am doing the next question and the door opens. Dad sticks his head in. "So you hate it here," he barks. I'm sure he'd talk to one of his patients better than that. I scrunch my shoulders to my ears, squeeze tears back — again — and cross to the closet mirror.

"Well, for starters they laugh at me." I point at my reflection in the mirror. "Look at my shoes, my dumb plaid skirt. And yellow sweater, for heaven's sake." I glare back at myself. "Janice, the other new girl in homeroom," — *with her big expanding chest*, I say in my head — "she wears a black, swirly skirt with a pink poodle on it and a tight, matching, pink angora sweater. And there's ugly" —

flat chested, I add again in my head — "me wearing this." I yank at my woollen pleats. "No wonder they call me a country bumpkin."

"Buck up, Nora. I don't want to hear any more of this nonsense." The door begins to close.

I raise my voice. "You don't know what it's like to be a girl." I watch my blotchy face, surrounded by straggly bits of mouse-brown hair sticking out from my equally straggly ponytail, disappear and reappear, as I move the sliding mirror door back and forth. "I need Mum. I want her back."

"We all do." He drums his fingers against the door frame. "But can't you be —"

"I know exactly what you're going to say," I interrupt. "You're like all the other adults." I curl my face up and mimic back to him. "Your mother would want you to be happy." I scowl into the mirror. "Well I'm not happy. So there." Dad scowls and sighs a bad-tempered sigh.

Then my mouth starts running away from my brain. Like it blurts out things that have been inside my head for weeks but couldn't say out loud. "The Sunday school teacher used to say that God could see whatever we do. If Mum's with God, can she see me? Are they both — her and God — watching me? I don't mean watching over. I mean watching, watching. Like can they see me when I do something wrong? When I'm mean?" I gulp in some air. "And why does God have to be a man?"

Dad has this weird sort of look. Like how could this person be my daughter? He sighs again and turns his head as if to go, then stops. He takes a deep breath. "No, I don't believe your mother is watching you. Or watching me, either. Some people may. I was told the same thing about

God when I was little, but now I think it's a way of trying to make children behave."

"And then there's this hair." I sweep back the stray ends with my hands and jam a bobby pin in place. "If the little ends don't droop over my eyes, they stand up. Like I'm going to lift off and fly away. Janice has curls that flounce and bounce, saying with each flounce and bounce, *Aren't I beautiful?* Why did they waste nice, red hair on the likes of you?"

Dad takes in another deep breath. Bigger this time. His face twists. "I don't have time for this. Stop it. You're working yourself up." He closes the door, hard. Then opens it. "I don't want to hear any more about it. Forget it and get back to your studies. Tomorrow will be better." This time the door slams shut. *Yeah, sure,* I say in my head. He's not twelve and alone and me. I hear his heavy footsteps march to the kitchen. "And clean up this mess."

"*Argh,*" I yell. I make fists and lift them to strike the mirror, but hold back. I'm confused — about me, about God, about Mum, about Heaven, about how to be me. And angry too — at God, at Mum, at Dad. At me?

I open my Autograph book. Mum gave it to me last Christmas and wrote the first entry.

> *December 25, 1958*
> *My Dear Nora,*
> > *First in your Album*
> > *First in your thoughts*
> > *First to be remembered —*
> > *Last to be forgot.*
>
> > > > *Mother*

• • •

Penticton
September 11, 1959

Dear Nora,

Why aren't you writing? Maybe I'm writing too soon and a letter from you will come tomorrow. It's just that your last one sounded so down I was hoping you'd be feeling better.

Mum, Dad, Jack, and Dougie and I went for our usual Saturday "adventure," as Dad calls it. I figure it's an adventure for them because they get to run all over the place while I sit around and read. This time Mum stayed back with me for some reason, which was nice. We had a picnic first and the boys and Dad went looking for mountain sheep while Mum and me (I guess I should say Mum and I but there's nobody here to correct my grammar) cleared up. At least it was sunny. We've had a few cloudy days, which I hate. They put me in bad humour. Mum read her new Agatha Christie murder mystery and I tried again to read *Anne of the Island*. The girls act silly. Do all girls act that silly when they're eighteen or nineteen? You should know with Dot and Jan. I know you won't be like that when you're eighteen or nineteen. I don't even like the chapter titles ("The Shadow of Change" is the first one). So why am I reading it?

Mum has been bugging me about practising the piano. I like piano but sometimes I wonder why I bother. I'm no way near as good as she is. Besides, what's the point? Who knows if I'll be around to use it. (I've never said that out loud before. You know what I mean, writing is sort of like saying something out loud.)

Sally (the girl who lives on the other side of Draper's orchard) and I went to the movies last Saturday. We saw *The Nun's Story*. It was okay. The only problem was coming home. I walk so slowly Sally got mad at me. What's so bad about walking slowly? You get to look at lots of things. Maybe mad's too strong a word. I know she really didn't want to go with me but none of her real friends were around.

Sometimes I don't like that I can't do stuff like everybody else. Like field hockey — in Physical Training the teacher is all so nicey nice and says golly-gee-whiz it would be SUCH a help if I'd keep score. Really, I'd rather be able to play. And hula hoop and swim. In fact, I think I'd rather have had polio. At least

I'd have a brace on my leg like Cora and others would think it was neat. Besides, I could whack someone with it if I was really cross.

I guess I'm cross today. I miss having you here.

Mum and I were talking about your mum. I knew Aunt Rita was a nurse but didn't know she had trained in Alberta. Mum said she and her were like your two sisters, really close. They did everything together — swimming, dancing, picking in the orchard in the summer. And when Aunt Rita went so far away to training Mum missed her terribly. She still misses her terribly. She said when they were both having us, they were especially close all over again.

I wonder if we will be that close when we grow up. That's interesting. I never usually think of me growing up.

See you soon, I guess.

> Yours, not as down in the
> dumps as I thought,
> Lizzie

4

"It's for me." Janet jumps off the couch towards the ring-ing telephone.

"No, it's Jerry. He said he'd call." Dorothy rounds the door from the bathroom, grabbing the receiver off the wall. She runs her fingers though her blonde hair and takes in a big quietening breath. "Mackenzie residence. Dorothy speaking." A scowl. "Yes, she's here."

Janet holds out her hand with an I-told-you-it'd-be-for-me look on her face.

Dorothy puts her hand over the receiver. "Bummer. It's for you." She rolls her eyes. "Who in the heck can be call-ing her?" *They forget I'm sitting at the dining room table researching a Social Studies project in the encyclopedia. My stupid sisters.*

"Bummer. The telephone's for you." This time she yells. "Hurry up, Nora. They haven't got all day."

"I only answer to Nora." I snatch the receiver from behind her. The curly cord stretches and dances.

"Hello. Nora speaking." I can't believe it. It's a

response to my advertisement at the library. Yesterday I took my books back and got out *Anne of the Island*. While I was there I put up a notice: *Grade eight girl on 11th Street would like babysitting job, weekends*. If I'm going to get new shoes or go back to Penticton, I figure I'll have to earn the money myself. "That's fine. Thursday at four-thirty. Just let me get a pencil, please." Dot hovers. I cover the receiver and grit my teeth. "Can't I have a telephone conversation in private?" I rummage in the desk drawer for paper. "Yes?" I scribble *523 East 8th Street* and repeat it into the receiver. "Thanks. I'll see you then." I paste the note to my chest and stomp to my room.

"What's going on?" Dad's johnny-on-the-spot when there's anything possibly negative involving me.

"What d'ya know. Bummer got a phone call." You'd think they'd say it quietly if they're going to talk like that.

"Don't you call her that. You know she doesn't like it. Maybe she has a friend."

I can't believe it. Dad is actually taking my side for a change.

• • •

The Quinns' house is old and rambling, several blocks south and east of our place, with a large back garden and rickety-pickety fence. Well, picket fence. I just like the rickety-pickety rhyme. Mrs. Quinn meets me at the door.

"Hi. I'm Mrs. Quinn. Come in, come in. You must be Nora." I shake out my blue umbrella. The white flowers on it squish and spread. "You look like a drowned rat." My stomach twinges. Mum always said that when I came in from swimming. "And this leech hanging from my leg is Colin."

"Hi, leech." I can't help grinning. He's so cute — big brown eyes and a black cowlick that stands bolt upright from his short-back-and-sides cropped head.

Colin grins back. "I'm Colin. And I'm three years old."

"You can't be. You're much bigger than that." I hand my coat to Mrs. Quinn. "You must be at least four."

Colin lets go of his mother's leg and stretches up tall. "When will I be four, Mummy?" He holds up five fingers.

"Not until January, dear."

"You know your numbers already?" I bend over and fold down his thumb. At the same time I step out of my rain boots.

Mrs. Quinn ushers me into the living room. "These are my other two scallywags, Maureen and Patricia. Two girls jump up and down on the chesterfield and bat each other with pillows, laughing.

"Girls, girls. This is Nora. She's coming to help us out on Saturdays. She won't want to look after you if you act like a bunch of orangutans."

I wonder if three kids will be too much. Even though I'm tall and in grade eight, I'm not thirteen until November because I skipped grade two. But four hours at fifty cents an hour — two dollars a week — is a gold mine. I think again of new shoes and a bus ticket to Penticton.

"As I told you on the phone, I work Saturdays from one to five at the five-to-a-dollar store. My sitter left a few weeks back. Her own mother needed more looking after so she had to quit. I've been trying to find a permanent sitter ever since."

I glance around as Mrs. Quinn speaks. Games and books and blankets are strewn over the floor and a small black-and-white TV sits in the corner. The girls stop jumping.

"This is Maureen, my middle one." The stocky girl's fine wisps of fire-engine red hair frame her face in front of long, thin braids. "And this is Patricia." She pauses a moment. "My eldest." She's much the same height as the first but thinnish, with light golden-red curls. I smile. Colin pulls at my leg.

"How much sitting have you done before?" Mrs. Quinn asks.

I'm sort of honest. "Not much, but I love kids." I bend down to Colin. "Just a moment. I have to talk to your mum. Then we can play." I straighten up. "I have two little cousins who I used to look after." But not completely honest. I omit to say Lizzie and I babysat together, only when we had to, and definitely not for money. "I do miss them."

"Three children can be a handful. Do you still think you want to try?" I nod. "Well, I'll leave you with them for an hour or so. I'll be in the kitchen. Let's see how you manage." Colin follows his mother out of the room. "No, no, dear. You stay here. I thought you wanted to play with Nora."

Patricia and Maureen gather round. I crouch down. "Now which one of you is which again?" Colin wiggles in for a cuddle.

"I'm Maureen and I am seven and a half. But I prefer to be called Reenie." This, the dimply dumpling with braids.

"Hi, Reenie." I hold out my hand. We shake. "And, by my great powers of deduction, you must be Patricia." The other child stands a bit apart.

"Yes, and she's not seven and a half. She's only seven years and three months. And Mum doesn't like her called Reenie. She says Maureen's such a beautiful name."

"Maybe I can call her Reenie when your mum isn't around? Do you like Patricia or something else for short?"

"Well, some of my friends call me Pat. And Patricia is okay. But I like Trisha best. That's what Dad calls me." She scowls at Maureen's equally fierce face.

"There you are then. When we're together, you're Trisha and Reenie. And how grown-up are you, Trisha?"

"Oh, I'm eight, but I'll be nine on March fourth." Despite their difference in hair and bone structure, the two girls are much alike. Broad, open faces with pale skin and masses of freckles.

"I wish I had a sister close to my age. My two big sisters are much older and just a year apart from each other too. They're the greatest friends." Still squatting, I run my hand over and over Colin's black cowlick. Each time it pops up again. *Unmanageable like the rest of him?* I wonder.

"Aren't you going to ask about me?" Colin takes my head between his hands and forces me to look straight at him.

"I guess you want me to talk to you, Colin. Do you go to school?"

He shakes his head. "I stay at Mrs. Jomori's. She has two baby girls. It's boring."

"Where's your dad?"

"He's a miner. He's away." Maureen grabs my arm and pulls me to the couch. "Let's jump some more."

If I want this job — and I know now I do for sure — I figure I'd best calm the kids down and clean up the mess.

"Let's build a fort." I pick up the two pillows and blankets strewn on the floor.

"Yay." Three voices chorus.

"How?" asks Patricia.

"First we tidy up, make space in the middle of the room. And then we build."

Over the next while the three children gather up the games and stack them in the corner with the books next to the TV. Meanwhile I straighten out the chesterfield and cushions, turn four chairs upside down in the middle of the room, and drape the blankets from the couch over the chair legs. We each choose a pillow as our sitting spot inside our new fort. I grab a battered blue copy of *The Littlebits* from the pile of books.

"Let's read a story." Colin curls up on my lap, thumb in mouth. Maureen and Patricia snuggle in on either side. From the way the girls sigh I know they like the book as much as I did at their age.

The door opens and closes. But I read on to the end of the chapter. Then I hush the girls with a finger and squeeze out from under Colin's droopy body to go find Mrs. Quinn.

In the kitchen, the table is set for four and a smell of something sweet comes from the oven. Mrs. Quinn looks up from her book with a smile. "You certainly have a way with them. The last girl I tried was older than you but they ran rings around her."

"Colin's asleep on the floor, Mrs. Quinn. In the fort."

"Thanks, dear. You've been great. But before we decide for sure, I'd like to talk to your mother."

I feel my face flush. "I don't have a mother." Mrs. Quinn

pauses, opens her mouth to say something but appears to change her mind.

"Then I can talk to your dad?"

"You can. But you don't need to. He'll say it's okay." *He doesn't really notice me*, I add to myself.

"I'll phone him anyway. You be here on Saturday then, let's see, a little early, so I can show you the routine. About a quarter after twelve. Is that okay?" I know I want the money and I know I'm going to like it here. "If it goes well this Saturday then you have the job for good. I'll check with my children, of course." She presses a fifty-cent piece into my hand. "That's for today. Thanks, dear. Can you see yourself out? I don't want Colin to sleep too long or he won't want to go to bed tonight."

"Say bye to them for me, then." I slip on my boots and raincoat and partially open the still-dripping umbrella. "See you Saturday. Oh, and thanks."

I hurry home up Moody Avenue. My head's in a busy cloud of counting all the money I'll have when I hear a man's roar.

"Get yourself back in here, now." Another roar. "If you don't, I'll give you something to complain about." This time some of the words are slurred. I look around. There's no one on the street but me. I'm scared. But then I see movement. A girl, curled up next to a forsythia bush. It looks like Dolores. It can't be, but it is.

5

On Monday, school is as boring as ever. Even Music, which I loved — and I really mean loved — in Penticton, is boring. Here, Mrs. Bramley strums on her autoharp and we're supposed to sing. Hardly anyone does, and if they do it's a half sing. She flings one arm about as if to work up some enthusiasm but still it's an off-key, pathetic effort. Well, what do you expect with songs with words like "Mares eat oats, and does eat oats, and little lambs eat ivy. A kid'll eat ivy too, wouldn't you?" In Penticton we used to sing songs from musicals.

Two summers ago our whole family went to see the movie *South Pacific* for Mum's birthday, the twelfth of August. We sang "Some Enchanted Evening" and "I'm Gonna Wash That Man Right Outta My Hair" for days after. Mum then bought the record for Janet's birthday a few weeks later, and the singing started all over again. I know every piece. At the end of the class, I almost say to Mrs. Bramley, if we sang something from *South Pacific* or *Oklahoma!* maybe the kids would sing. But then I think, *Nah. If we do sing songs like that, I'll cry remembering.*

Right after Music is Physical Training, PT for short. It's my most hated class. It's not that I don't like to run or exercise or play soccer. I do. It's that I can't be invisible. In all my other classes, I go about my business, head down, and they go about theirs. Here it's different. I stick out because I'm pretty hopeless. Like, if we play field hockey, I trip over the stick. If we play soccer, my kick misses the ball and I stumble and nearly fall on my face. Dad said last year it's because I'm long and skinny and growing so fast. Surely that can't go on forever. Maybe I'm just uncoordinated and clumsy. Either way, it doesn't help when people are giggling behind their hands.

After class, it's even worse. We have to have a shower, but not if we have our period. Today, Margo Latimer says, "Please, Mrs. Grantham, will you excuse me from showering?" The other girls tee-hee.

Then someone invariably says to me, "Of course *you* have to take a shower." They tee-hee some more. Of course I have to. It's written all over my flat chest. There's more sniggering. What they're really saying is, *Too bad you're so immature.* So what's so great about getting your period, especially when they call it "the curse"? Nothing. At least not the way Dot whines and moans.

All this to say, nothing much has changed in three weeks at Sutherland Junior High. Except maybe I'm getting better at ignoring them. Well, not really. Even if I ignore them, I can't forget. What I really want is Mum back, Mum to hug me and tell me I'm special the way she used to. Dad doesn't even know I'm here.

Actually, maybe he would if I didn't make meals when I'm supposed to. Just a thought. When I get home I scrawl a new message on my chalkboard.

If I stop making meals
will you play with me
the way you used to,
Dad?

• • •

After school I go next door. The back steps of the Rev. and Mrs. Jim Taylor's house are painted in thick layers of grey. It's like if the sun dares to dry and lift the paint or a wayward shoe dares to chip it, more paint is slapped on. The Taylors themselves look grey. Just like I imagine a Reverend and Mrs. would look. And inside their house, everything is prim and proper, with doilies on side tables and the good china imprisoned in neat piles behind the glass doors of the buffet. There might as well be *No Touching* signs in every corner.

Despite their kid-unfriendly house and her hard and boney look, Mrs. Taylor is okay. She's invited me over to see her cat, Fluffy, who's having kittens. The cat has long black hair with a splash of white under her chin.

As far as I'm concerned, Fluffy is the most boring name imaginable for a cat. So I call her Carmody instead. But I don't say so in front of Mrs. Taylor. Just like I won't use the word pregnant again. I did once. Mrs. Taylor looked at me and said with her thin-lipped, cold voice, "Proper girls do not use words like that."

"Like what?" I asked.

She cleared her throat. Her voice came out raspy. "Words referring to our bodies and private matters."

My doctor dad uses all sorts of words. I kind of know you don't go around saying penis and vagina and breast in public, but I'm really not sure what's wrong with pregnant. Isn't that how we all got here? Anyway, that tells you something about Mrs. Taylor.

The point of all this is that Fluffy/Carmody is going to have kittens really soon. I would like to be there when she has them, but I haven't asked Mrs. Taylor. I don't think she'd be for it, given I have to be protected even from words like pregnant. But I figure my odds for being present for the birth are much higher if I go to the Taylors' really often. The cat bed is on the outside back porch so that's easy.

Today there's another girl next door. She's Mrs. Taylor's niece and she's nine. Her name is Stella. We sit on the porch. First I pat Carmody, then she pats Carmody. The cat purrs warm and soft. We purr too, a human-type purr. Stella tells me about her big bossy sister, Lori. I tell her my big sisters are bossy too. I don't tell her about Mum. And she doesn't ask.

When I leave for home, Stella says, "Will you be here tomorrow?"

"Probably."

"See yah then." It feels nice. Like I have a friend. But being only nine, she's not a real friend.

I want new shoes
I want a real friend
I want to go back to Penticton

• • •

43

I open my autograph book:

> *To my best friend Nora,*
> *Out in the ocean*
> *On a little rock —*
> *Three little words*
> *"Forget me not."*
>
> > *Love and good thoughts,*
> > *Vicki Matthews*

Has she forgotten me already?

• • •

Penticton
September 22, 1959

Dear Nora,

Thanks for your letter. I received it right
after I mailed my last one. You still don't
sound happy. Why not? You get to be
in the big city and not in this dump of
a town. But then I wasn't very happy in
my last letter, if I remember correctly.

I've changed my mind about Mrs.
Cramer. She's really unfair. In homeroom
some of the guys are so stupid. And
because of that she now jumps on all of
us if we barely move. Her son (do you
remember Billy Cramer?) is in my Math
and Science classes and he's weird or dumb

44

or both. There must be something wrong
— I mean really wrong — with him, the
way he acts. Mind you, it must be awful to
have your mother as a teacher, especially
when kids don't like her. Or at least I don't.

I play the guessing game with Dougie and Jack much more now that you're
not here. Tonight it was the planets and
stars and moons and stuff from *World
Book*. The boys are either really smart
or have great memories. Miss Banks,
Jack's first-grade teacher (we had her too,
remember?), stopped Mum downtown
on Saturday. Apparently Miss Banks had
pointed to the letter *q* over the blackboard at school and said it's always fol-
lowed by a *u*. Jack's hand shot up. "What
about Qatar?" Isn't that a hoot? I bet her
face was red. The boys and I had been
looking at a map of the Middle East a
few nights earlier. I think they're going
to be extra really smart because, with
you not here, I have nothing to do but
teach them things.

I'm telling you a secret. A secret
from Mum and Dad, that is. Everybody
in the whole school almost knows, so I
guess it isn't a secret. I couldn't get up
the stairs at school today. You know the
big stairs at the side of the building we
always go into? Well, at about step four,

I just knew I couldn't get to the top. I was panting and my breathing was really shallow. It was scary. The principal and Miss Dale took my arms and helped me to the classroom. They tried to make me go to the nurse's room but I said *no*. I knew they would phone Mum if I did. It was *soooo* embarrassing. I could see kids whispering behind their hands.

Don't you dare tell Uncle Alan or Janet or Dorothy.

I'm finding *Anne of the Island* pretty dull. Maybe Mum was right that it's too old for me. That Philippa Gordon is so silly, and all the girls (except Anne) ever talk about is boys. I only read it when I have nothing else to read. I had to renew it.

I guess I'm in a bad mood again. Jenny is back from her holiday *finally*, but I don't like her much anymore. She's really stuck-up. She got to drive to Ontario in the summer. Somehow it makes her better than us. I don't know why. Anyway, I usually hang around with Clara and Molly now but that's not the same as with the old Jenny or you.

Write soon.

Your cousin,
Lizzie

PS Don't you dare tell.

It's the same every lunch hour. It's like I always choose the table with a *Do Not Eat Here* sign. Except I'm the only one who can't read the message. So I eat alone. Kids jam around the large tables of the cafeteria. But nobody comes to the table I sit at. I cram the food in, grab my binder, pitch my brown paper lunch bag in the garbage can, and go walkies. That's what I call it. I stride to one end of the school like I'm going to the library, round the corner where nobody is, make an about-face, and stride in the opposite direction. I am *soooo* busy, *soooo* important that I can't even stop to chat.

Every day is the same. Except today. And I'd rather have it normal. Today Dolores and her friend Trudy are around the corner where I usually turn.

"Hiya. Saw you in the park with some kids on Saturday." It's Dolores, the one I call Black Hair/Kiss Curl in my head.

"Yup," I say.

"Are they your brother and sisters?" Bobby pins holding her kiss curls in place, she's got the usual heavy makeup on that makes her look like, I don't know, a cross between a clown and a movie star. I would say prostitute but I don't think I'm supposed to know about that stuff. Imagine if I used that word in front of Mrs. Taylor.

"Could be." I'm not sure why I don't tell them the truth. Is it because they'll tell everyone at school and then they'll all avoid me or talk behind my back? But then they already do.

"We've changed our minds. You can be our friend now. You can walk down Lonsdale with us after school. We usually stop for pop and a donut."

"Some other time." I walk on to the school library, find a table, and pretend to study. No one's there but the librarian, reading and munching on an apple.

• • •

It's after supper. The phone rings. I ignore Dad's yell from the basement. The ringing continues. I hear him thump up the stairs. "Hi there, Mary." Pause. "Of course. Of course." Pause. "Maybe that's a good thing." Pause. "We look forward to it. I'll pick you up at the station. See you Tuesday night." Then a clunk of the receiver on the hook.

"Nora." Dad's voice goes up at the end when he expects me to come to him, chop chop. Fast fast. He's in the kitchen, reading glasses in one hand, stroking his non-existent beard with the other. The light from the dining room is glinting off his glasses onto the wall.

"That was sure short, Dad."

"So if you could hear it was short, why couldn't you hear the phone ring and answer it?"

I open my mouth. My brain is not in gear. Again.

"Uh, I didn't want to." It comes out snippy.

"Quit that, Nora. Why are you so bad-tempered all the time?"

"Me, bad-tempered? It takes one to know one, Dad. You're the bad-tempered person around here."

If Dad had hair running down his neck and back, it would be standing straight up, like on a ferocious dog. Why does my mouth say such things?

"Don't talk back to your elders."

"I'm not talking back. I'm stating the facts."

"Well, I am tired of your being in the dumps all the time. Snap out of it."

"I don't know why you say that. I make supper every night. I do the dishes. I help with the laundry and I'm only twelve. No kids I know do that much." Of course, I don't know anybody here, but certainly Lizzie and my other friends in Penticton don't. *And what do you do most of the time,* my mind continues, *but stay in your room in the basement?*

"Oh, never mind." He waves his hand in front of his face like he's waving away an annoying mosquito. "That was your Aunt Mary on the phone. She and Lizzie are coming down next week for a few days. Lizzie has to have some tests."

"Great." I grin and fly back into my room, reach under my pillow for my Autograph book and read where it falls open.

> *To my friend Nora,*
> *When you get married and live in a tree,*
> *Send me a coconut COD.*
> *Clara — hope you like North Van*

Dear Nor,
> *When you get old and out of shape,*
> *remember girdles are only $4.98.*
>> *Love, Molly Johnson*

Remember, Nora,
> *Kiss beneath the garden gate,*
> *Kiss beneath the rose,*
> *But the proper place to kiss a boy ...*
> *is right beneath the nose.*
>> *Cora*

Silly, silly, silly. But I feel warmer inside remembering. I can see the pencil rub-out where Cora spelled my name with an *h* by mistake.

To my darling niece, Nora,
> *Oranges grow in Florida,*
> *California, too.*
> *But it takes a place like Penticton*
> *To grow a peach like you.*
>> *Love, Aunt Mary*

I smile knowing they will be here soon.

• • •

It's now Saturday and my second official time at the Quinns'. Last week we went to the park. There were swings, slides, a teeter-totter, monkey bars, and a sandbox. The swings are for big kids so I held Colin on my lap.

Colin hollered, "Higher, Nor, higher," while I pumped and pumped until it felt like we were going over the top.

But today it's pouring. Again. So, with bits of old clothes and material I'd rummaged from our basement, I'm making clothes for each of the kids' dolls, all by hand. Mrs. Quinn doesn't have a sewing machine.

Patricia's Raggedy Ann doll is called Annie and Maureen's is Rannie. I thought the names were cute when I first heard them, but now I think they're dumb and annoying. Both dolls live up to the word *raggedy*. I cut out a green skirt and blouse for one and plaid skirt and blouse for the other. I pin and baste tiny stitches as the girls look on, all eyes.

"When I've finished them, Annie and Rannie can share them, just like real sisters."

"How did you learn to do that?" Patricia is always the one to ask the questions.

"My Mum. She made doll clothes for me when I was little and then showed me how to make them when I got bigger." *Do you remember, Mum?*

"Brixton wants a sweater." Colin shoves forth his teddy bear.

"Sorry, I don't have wool for a sweater. And I'm no good at knitting." I find some heavy brown material that was Dad's pants. "How about a coat? Will this do?"

The afternoon races by. The children are pretty patient as I invent outfits. When they get wiggly we play I spy.

"I spy something that's yellow." The curtains in the kitchen.

"I spy something that's brown and green." The carpet in the living room.

"I spy something that begins with *p*." I say it like puh, not the name of the letter, so Colin is included. I'm thinking of the picture on the mantelpiece of Patricia and Maureen with an older girl. Maureen guesses the answer, but Patricia adds in a whispery voice. "That's our sister, Beatrice. She died."

"Oh, that's terrible." What do I say? Why do people die? It's not fair. "When did she die?" I poke fiercely at the cloth with my needle. "Ouch."

"A while ago."

I suck the flesh of my left thumb. Beatrice looks to be ten or eleven, and Maureen and Patricia, maybe four and five.

Colin clutches at me. "I'm not in the picture, am I?"

"No, pet, you're not." I blink back tears and shove the coat for the teddy bear into my own bag. It will need sewing on a machine for strength.

"What's wrong?" Colin cuddles in close, gives me a hug.

"Nothing. Well, no ... yes ... well, really I'm thinking of my mum." It's so hard to say. To say out loud. "She died too."

"You don't have a mummy?" Patricia and Maureen fling their arms around me. "Oh, that's awful."

"You must miss her."

"I can't imagine not having mummy."

I freeze. I shove the needle and thread into the sewing box and stand up. "Anyway, this is all the sewing for today." I wipe my eyes with my sleeve.

Colin pulls at my legs. "Why doesn't she come back, Nor?" His voice is high pitched.

"Don't be silly, Colin. She's dead. Like Bea." Maureen shoves aside his arms and gives me a big squeeze. "We miss Bea. At least, Trisha and I do. He was too little."

"Will my mummy die too?"

"No, Col. She'll be around for a long, long time to help you grow up to be a big man." I mentally cross my fingers. How do I say the right thing? "Let's clean up now and see if it has stopped raining." I look at the clock. "Oh my goodness, your mum'll be home any minute." I rush around picking up bits of thread and cloth, flinging them into the garbage can. The door opens.

"I'm home."

"Mum, look what Nora made." Colin runs to the door, holding up pyjamas for his bear.

"What a great babysitter you have." She beams at me. I feel my insides warm.

"Mummy," Colin pulls at his mother's leg, "Nora doesn't have a mummy, just like we don't have a big sister. They died."

"Did she really? Oh, that's terrible." Mrs. Quinn hands me my babysitting money. I shove it into my sweater pocket.

"Bye, everyone." I want out as quickly as possible.

Mrs. Quinn grabs the door and closes it behind us, just as fast. She's on the front steps with me. The rain's bouncing off the sidewalks, running in currents down the road.

"Nora, dear. I can't imagine losing your mum when you're just a girl. But I do know what it is like to be a mum and lose a daughter. If you ever want to talk about it, I'm here."

I paste on a smile. "Thanks, Mrs. Quinn." Each drop of rain zings my face, bounces, splashes, and dribbles down. Is it only rain on my cheeks?

I open my umbrella with a snap.

7

It's Sunday supper time and I have to ask.

"Dad, what's wrong with Lizzie?" We've just finished eating heated-up, leftover roast beef and mashed potatoes Jan and Dot made last night. I cooked carrots to go with them. There will be enough meat for sandwiches for half the week. I like that. Dad unfolds his reading glasses and sets his newspaper to the side.

"You mean her health?"

I nod. *What else?* I say in my head. "I know you used to call her a blue baby. But what does that mean?"

Dad pulls his pipe from his pocket and tamps it down. "I could tell something was wrong right from the beginning, when she was first born. With my stethoscope on her chest, I heard an odd murmur, like a swoosh instead of the normal *kethud kethud*. I knew she must have a hole in her heart or have valves not working properly." He sucks in as he lights his pipe. "The technical word for it is Tetralogy of Fallot."

"Dad, why are you doing that?" I stare at the pipe. "You

stopped smoking. You know Mum doesn't like you doing that." His face blanches. "Didn't," I add.

He puffs twice more and cradles the pipe in his hands. A curl of whiteness sweeps up and over his face. Why has he started smoking again?

"I was pretty sure that's what she had and I was worried for a whole month until you were born that there might be something wrong with you, too. I didn't tell your mother." He twiddles the pipe in his hands.

"But Dad, Lizzie had an operation before. She already has a huge scar all across her front to right up under her arm. Didn't that fix it?" I ladle out Aunt Mary's home-canned cherries into two bowls and put the half empty jar in the refrigerator.

"Only a bit. That's all they could do then and even that operation was really new. They had only been performing it for a couple of years."

"You mean she was experimented on?"

"Not really." He tips the half-burned tobacco from his pipe onto a plate. The smoke wisps up. It has a sweet smell. "They had done lots of those procedures on animals and a few on children. I'm not sure how many."

"So, what exactly did they do?" I slurp a mouthful of cherries and carefully spit out the pits onto my spoon.

"Because of the hole, the blood on the right side in the heart, which is low in oxygen, mixes with the blood on the left side, which is full of oxygen. Therefore, the blood sent to the lungs has more oxygen in it than it should."

"What do you mean? I thought you want your blood to have lots of oxygen." More mouthfuls of cherries. More pits piling up on the side plate.

"You do — going to the rest of your body. But the blood going to your lungs should have mostly carbon dioxide, so that when you breathe in, the oxygen from the air can get exchanged for the carbon dioxide. That way you continue to get more fresh oxygen in your blood." I listen hard. The to-and-from directions are very confusing. "Then that blood goes back from the lungs to your heart and is pumped to the rest of your body. You want the blood that goes to your lungs to have lots of carbon dioxide in it, not lots of oxygen." Giving the bowl of his pipe a few more upside down taps on the plate, Dad checks that it's completely empty and places the pipe in his shirt pocket. "Is that clear?"

"Not really." I busy myself, removing the dirty dishes from the table. It gives me a chance for what he said to sink in. Maybe. I bring back the steeped tea and place the pot next to Dad's untouched dessert bowl. "But what did they do for Lizzie in her first operation?"

"They put in what's called a shunt. They separated a branch of one of her arteries here," he runs his hand up his chest towards his neck, "and connected it with the artery that takes blood to her lungs. That artery didn't have much oxygen in it, relatively speaking, so they sent it back again to the lungs to get more oxygen." He cups his hands on either side of his rib cage.

"You mean so she has more oxygen for her brain?"

"That's right. And everywhere else. When she had that operation, it was meant to help only until they figured out how to fix the major problem, the hole in the middle of her heart. What it did was give her time to grow bigger and time for surgeons to work out how to help her more."

"Why haven't they done it before?" I push Dad's cherries closer to him. "You should eat your fruit, Dad." I sound like my mother.

"Because they couldn't. They didn't know how." He dives into the cherries. "But antibiotics and new operating techniques have been developed in the last little while." His words come out garbled through a full mouth. "Mmmm. These cherries are good. I told your Aunt Mary when you girls were little, the longer Lizzie stays healthy and the longer she can wait to have her operation, the better. Even now they've only done a few operations in Canada, let alone here in Vancouver, like the one she'll need. It's still very, very new. Each year the surgeons get more skilled and each year the nurses, the other doctors will know more about how to look after her during and after the operation."

"So I was right. They're experimenting on her."

"I don't like to think of it as experimenting. But, in a way you're correct, because with each operation they get better. Then the chance for it to work the next time, on the next girl or boy, increases." He wipes his cherry-stained mouth with a serviette.

"So this time they're going to open up her heart and sew up the hole?"

Dad nods. "I don't know actually how they do it, but yes."

"Without this operation will Lizzie die?" I hate to use the *d* word but somehow I must.

"Let's not talk about that." He wipes his face again, harder.

"Dad, I have to know, and I don't want it watered down." It's like I have to hurt myself, jab the knife in. But that's better than not knowing.

Dad's face twists as he screws his serviette into a ball and rams it half under his dessert bowl.

"Yes, dear. Without another operation she will die. Sooner rather than later."

I look across at Dad. Most of what he says I don't understand, like where the arteries are, where the carbon dioxide is. But this part, I do. The silence in the room is heavy. My ears roar and close in. My mind wants to close in too, but can't. How can Lizzie die? The air is thick and wavy, like looking through water. She can't die. She's young. She can't. But the Quinn girl did. Beatrice did.

I reach for the teapot and slide my hands up and down. It's warm and comforting. "You said she'll be one of the first to have it?" Dad nods. "Will they fix her? Will it work?"

This time he doesn't nod. "From what I've read, there's a good chance."

"You mean, even if she has it, it might not help? She might be just the same?" He nods again. His face twists and pinches more.

"And what if it doesn't work?"

"Let's not talk about that, dear." He gathers up his half-finished cup of tea and starts for the kitchen.

"No, please Dad. I want to know. I have to know."

The cup plunks on the countertop. With a hold-on-a-second look on his face, he heads for downstairs. I don't move.

I remember how Lizzie never used to run and play. At the beach in the summer she read while, I jumped in and out of the water, swam for a while and then dripped down beside her. Lizzie sometimes paddled, ducked under, rolled onto her back, but she didn't swim, not out to the raft to dive off. She went back to her book instead. I always thought she didn't run or swim because she preferred to read. But now that I think about it, I did know it was about her shortness of breath and the scar on her chest.

"These are copies of the *Canadian Medical Association Journal*." I startle. Dad's back with a thick book under his arm and several thin, magazine-like things, with pieces of paper sticking out from one end.

"When will she have the new operation?" I ask.

Dad flips through the journals, then leafs through the book. It seems to be some sort of medical encyclopedia. "Look here." It's a diagram labelled "Circulation of the Blood through the Heart." He drags his fingers on one side of the picture into an upper area that looks like the bag on our vacuum cleaner, then to a lower bag, and out what looked like pipes. "Blood comes from all of the cells of our body to our heart. It carries, among other things, lots of carbon dioxide that our body needs to get rid of."

"Then it gets pumped to the lungs?" I point to those big pipes at the top.

"You bet. Those are our pulmonary arteries. They carry the blood full of carbon dioxide from the heart to the lungs. There we breathe in oxygen and that gets exchanged for the carbon dioxide. See." He drags his finger along what looks like more pipes and back through other sack-like things. "Then it comes through this upper area, called the left atrium, down into the left ventricle, and out the aorta to all the rest of the body."

"That's really amazing, Dad."

"The amazing thing is that the heart has to work and pump the blood every second of our lives."

"So where's the hole in Lizzie's heart?"

Dad points to the area between the two lower sacks. "Lizzie has a big hole — about the size of a fifty-cent piece is what they say — in the wall between the two ventricles, these two bottom parts." He pauses again for me to let it sink in.

"Here?" I point to the line in the diagram running down the middle of the heart, then sit back thinking. "Oh, I see. So the blood in one side with mostly carbon dioxide could mix with the blood in the other side that has the oxygen."

"Clever girl." Dad smiles. I like it when he smiles. His freckles seem to skitter all over his face.

"But with Lizzie, the blood she sends to the rest of her body has less oxygen in it than it should, so she doesn't have the energy to run or jump or play?"

"Exactly."

"How will you know when she should have the operation?"

"I told you. Every month they know more. Every month they're getting better at operations on the heart. The longer we wait, the better."

"Yeah, but how would you know when she really has to have it. Like, she can't not have it or it will be too late." My voice cracks.

Dad scratches his head and runs his left hand down the back of his neck. His dark, reddish hair has an occasional streak of grey. "Well, I suppose when she can't go to school any longer. Or can't walk very far without stopping. I'm only guessing. I'm not the specialist. I wish I were so I could help her more. But I don't think they would want to leave it until she couldn't walk at all. She might be too weak for the operation itself." It's like he's talking to himself.

I think back to Lizzie's letter. *Don't you dare tell your dad.* But they're coming down for tests so the doctors will find out. I can't tell Dad. I'm sure it's no big deal. *It is, isn't it, Mum? No big deal?*

• • •

Penticton
September 26, 1959

Dear Nor,

Why don't you write more often? I asked Vicki if you'd written lately. She said *no*. Is it that bad? If you're lonely, isn't it helpful to write? Or are you so busy with all your new friends and all the sports and stuff? I forgot you said there wasn't much in the way of sports for girls at your school. Is there something for girls to do, like a choir?

Mum did find out about me not being able to go up the stairs. Since then I've been fine, I told her. But she phoned the doctor anyway. I don't know what that means. I am more tired. Mum has to wake me every morning. And after school, I'm really slow walking up our long driveway. I have to stop and catch my breath. I let Dougie and Jack run ahead but I don't think Mum knows that.

I'm looking forward to seeing you. But not looking forward to being in the hospital. My memory of staying there when I was five is pretty vague. They cut me open all around my chest, and even low down on my stomach, to put in a shunt that's sort of like a pipe, they said, and fix some valves. You've seen the scars. But mostly I remember the loneliness of being left with strangers, even though Mum and Aunt Alice came every day. I remember a nurse with a large, wide-brimmed cap who swept in and out of the room like a boat in full sail. I'm sure she was kind, or at least okay, but I still can feel the fear. I wonder why.

But the bus ride to Vancouver will be great. I'll have Mum all to myself. I never get to be with her much because of the boys. We can read and talk and stare out the window. She says the leaves might be pretty in Manning Park. Sorry. You don't get to be with your mum at all. That was thoughtless of me.

Hope you're fine and all my worrying about you is for nothing. I will stamp this and send Dougie to the mail box.

Your favourite cousin (I'd better be),
Lizzie

PS I took *Anne of the Island* back to the library. I didn't finish it. Ooops, I think I told you that in my last letter. Or did I?

8

I fold Lizzie's letter into my pocket. I always re-read her letters — sometimes over and over and over. I'm glad, really glad, Lizzie knows she's insensitive about wanting to talk more with her mum. Because she is. Was. She should be sorry. She should know better. At school I overhear kids saying nasty things about their mums and I get furious. I want to yell at them, *Don't you realize how lucky you are to have a mum?* or, *No matter how bad she is it's better than having no mum.* But I don't. They'd all look at me like I'm a fool, and they'd find out about Mum. I am glad I told the Quinns, though. It feels like I don't have to hold myself in quite the same.

One more day until Lizzie comes. I wonder if she's changed since the summer. Will she look different?

I skim through the letter a fourth time and pause on the part about Lizzie looking forward to being with her mother. I feel the tears well up again. Why do I have to be such a sop? No one else cries. Is there something wrong with me?

To my friend Nora,
Honey in the morning
Honey in the night
Honey in the afternoons
And everything's all right.

Micki Arase

Everything is not all right.

• • •

On Tuesday I make it home from school in seventeen minutes. I run up the back steps two at a time. Aunt Mary's in the kitchen washing the breakfast porridge pot. I wrap myself around her in a huge hug. "Oh, it's so good to see you. To see someone from home. Where's Lizzie?"

"Lying down. Travelling is tiring. Oooh, I'm going to get porridge-y water all over you."

"Can Lizzie and I sleep in Jan and Dot's room and you sleep in my room?" I hop up and down.

"Hold on. Calm down." Aunt Mary upturns the pot on the wire rack and wipes her hands on her apron. Now she squeezes me in a rocking sort of way. "I don't see why not, as long as you girls sleep. You have school tomorrow and Lizzie has her tests." She turns back to the counter. "But your dad should be the one to say."

"We'll sleep. I promise." I give my aunt another hug from behind. "I just can't wait. When can I see Lizzie?" I dump my school bag on the floor under the telephone.

"If she's awake she'll have heard you come in." Aunt Mary unwraps some beets and onions from old newspapers.

Clumps of dirt fall away. "First let me hear what you're doing at school."

I feel my shoulders sink as I plop down on a kitchen stool. "Not much. I hate school. I miss Penticton and you and Lizzie and my friends there."

"What about friends here?"

"I don't have any. No one talks to me."

"Do you talk to them? Do you smile?"

"Why should I? They laugh at me, at my shoes, at my clothes."

Aunt Mary pushes aside the beets, washes her hands, wipes them on her apron, leaving a pinky dirt stain, and puts the kettle on the stove. I can tell from the slow, careful action that she's going to say something. It reminds me of Mum. "How about a cup of tea? You like tea, don't you, with lots of milk?"

I tuck my feet up on the seat of the chair, fold my arms around my legs, and nod. I can't help staring at Aunt Mary. It's like looking at Mum. I never noticed before. They have the same dark hair, the same cute ski-jump noses, the same twinkly eyes. Hers are blue but Mum's were brown. I feel my eyes well. Again.

"Oh, Aunt Mary, seeing you makes me miss Mum all the more."

She pours boiling water into the teapot. "It's the same for me, Nora. You look just like your mum when she was your age." My eyes widen, my head cocks to one side. "But it's wonderful too. Because it's a little bit like having Rita back. We were sisters but, don't forget, we were also best friends."

I pour tea into my mug. Then into my aunt's. "And you sound exactly like Mum."

"The four of us girls, my sisters and I, we were close. I love Alice and Beth, but they're older." Mary pours milk into both mugs. "That okay?" She nods to my milky tea. "But Rita and I were less than two years apart. And because we were both tall and strong we got to do the picking in the orchard, not having brothers and all." Aunt Mary sips her steamy tea, eyes smiling off into the distance. "Then we'd run all the way down the hill to the beach to swim, climb half the way up again, turn around, and go back down because we were already hot, laughing all the way. Meanwhile, Alice and Elisabeth were in the house helping mother with supper. I used to begrudge the time they got to be with her. It's crazy because, despite the hard work of picking, I wouldn't have wanted to be indoors all the time either."

Hearing about Mum when she was young, I feel my loneliness lift.

"You have that same long and lean body that she had, the same hair." She pauses. "Is there something wrong with the tea?"

"No, no. It's good." I come back to the present, add more milk, and slurp. "But my hair isn't like Mum's. Hers was dark. Mine's a mousy brown."

"Hers was like that too at your age but became a deep chestnut colour later. She wore it long, in a French braid. Really lovely."

"Could you do my hair up like that tomorrow morning?"

Aunt Mary empties her teacup. "How about tomorrow night we can have a girl session of doing each other's hair. Maybe you can even practise the French braid on yourself."

I uncurl and give my aunt another hug. "I'm glad you're here. Dad never talks to me about Mum or Penticton.

Even what he's doing. Sometimes I don't think he knows I'm around."

Aunt Mary pushes me out of our hug, holds me by both shoulders, and looks me straight in the eye. "Don't forget your dad misses Rita too."

"But he talks to Dot and Janet."

"Maybe he thinks you're too young — which you aren't — or maybe you remind him too much of your mother. And some men don't like to talk about feelings, you know. They think they have to be strong all the time — which is silly — and they think crying means they're not — which is also silly."

"No one even mentioned Mum on her birthday."

"Oh, my dear. I thought of it but just imagined you people were having a special evening to yourselves." Aunt Mary gives me another hug. A long, long squeeze. "I'm so sorry. I should have called."

"What did she die of?" I look up at her from our hug. I don't want to let her go.

"Didn't you know? A type of cancer called leukemia."

"I'm sure they told me but things didn't stick in my brain very well back then. It was so fast." Ooops. Here come the tears again.

"Don't forget we're all sad but we handle it in different ways. That includes your sisters. Maybe you just have to tell your dad that you need to talk to him, about school and about your mother. I can certainly mention to him about your clothes and shoes. Lots of times men don't understand the importance of clothes for girls." Aunt Mary untangles my arms and turns back to the counter. "But I've got to get a move on and make this soup. Which do you want to do — chop the beets or the onions?" She pulls out the under-the-counter cutting board and hands me a knife. You like beet soup don't you? And apple crumble? Lizzie and I brought as many apples from our tree as we could fit into our suitcases." Aunt Mary gives me a broad smile and an unexpected hug. Actually, the hugs are all somewhat unexpected because our family is not usually the huggiest in the world. I wish we were. I can never get too many hugs.

"Yes and yes. I like them both. And I'll chop the beets — the onions will make me cry." I curl up my mouth in a half grin. "And I don't need any more help with that than I already have."

"Speaking of Lizzie, look what the cat dragged in."

• • •

That evening Lizzie and I run next door — well Lizzie doesn't run, it's more of a go-next-door slowly — and check out Fluffy/Carmody to see if she is still kitten-less. She is. While we hand her back and forth, stroke her and listen to the responding purr, we chatter about Penticton and school and Jenny and Vicki and homework until it gets late. Then we curl up in the twin beds in the basement and play our usual word game. One person whispers a word, the other a word it reminds them of, going back and forth until we either fall asleep or burst out laughing at the silliness. But tonight it neither sends us to sleep nor into gales of laughter.

"How are you really?" It's Lizzie who breaks the silence.

"Really really?"

"Yes, really really."

"About school, you mean?"

"Well, maybe. I also mean about Aunt Rita."

"I don't know. I thought moving here would be easier. The kids in Penticton all treated me like I had some sort of disease. Mother-dying disease, I guess. Like they'd catch it. No one asked what it was like for me. The only person who really said anything was Marion Carmichael. She cried at Mum's funeral and kept saying, 'I'm *soooo* sorry,' over and over. I yelled at her. 'It was my mum who died not yours. So why are you crying?' I guess that wasn't very nice."

"It's hard to know what to say."

"Yeah." *Like at the Quinns'*, I think.

"And we don't want the same thing to happen to our mothers."

"Sometimes at night I can't even see her face any more. Oh, Lizzie! I'm scared I'll forget her."

There's silence in the room except for the tick of the alarm clock and creak of floor boards above.

9

Friday after school I trudge down Lonsdale Avenue with Dolores and Trudy. Half the time I stare at the others' feet as they skip around puddles and I wonder why I'm here. Lizzie and Aunt Mary went back this morning and I'm already looking forward to their return.

The air is heavy with moisture, but it's not raining any more. The first time in days. I draw to the side to avoid the splash of grimy water from passing cars. Boys eye Dolores as we pass. She dips her head and flaps her eyelids a little faster than usual.

In the café, Trudy and Dolores plunk their coats and books in the booth and shove in facing each other. I stand there feeling foolish. "Oh yeah, you're here." Dolores gets up. I scrunch in next to the wet coats. "We're getting a Coke and jelly donut," says Dolores. "You too?"

"Just an Orange Crush."

"No donut? Getting too fat, are yah?" Does she like being mean? The last thing anyone could call me is fat, but I still flush.

"I'm saving my money." Why did I say that?

"What for?"

"To go back to Penticton. I don't like it here." I should've said, to get away from you guys. Get away from the unending rain, rain, rain. Or, should've said we're going on a holiday to France. Or Australia. Or England.

Trudy's eyes widen. "You'd go back to Penticton by yourself? What about your family?"

"I don't have much family here." Oh, why did I say that as well?

"I thought those kids were your little sisters."

"And brother," adds Dolores.

"Nope." Say nothing.

"So who were they?"

"Who cares?"

"Then why don't you like it here?"

"That's a dumb question. Why do you think?"

"'Cause the kids don't like you?"

"Because most of them are snooty."

"They think you're snooty." Trudy sucks on her straw too hard. Fizz goes up her nose and she screws up her face. "Wasn't it Jeannie Cruikshank who said that? Or was it Alvina?"

"Imagine having a name like that, Alvina. I hear their parents wanted a boy named Alvin. So she had to be Alvina." Dolores circles her tongue around her lips to take in the crumbs of donut glaze. "How would you feel not being wanted because you're a girl?"

"That's not nice. Maybe they didn't know they were having twins and picked out a boy's name and a girl's name." I swirl my straw round and round the lip of the glass. Good change of topic. "Didn't your mother and father tell you if you can't say something nice don't say it?"

"Oooh. Aren't we just little Miss Goody Two-Shoes." Dolores stands up. "I'm going to the washroom. Coming, Trude?"

I stare into the blank air in a café full of kids. What am I doing here? Sitting. Waiting.

Like waiting in the hospital to see Mum. I sat there in the hall for what seemed like forever, hoping to sneak into her room when the head nurse wasn't around. You have to be thirteen to visit someone in the Penticton hospital. Dorothy and Janet were old enough, but not me. One time Dad came along and said, "Come on, Nora girl. I don't care what the rules are, you're seeing your mother." I crawled up on the bed with Mum. We hugged and hugged until I didn't have the strength in my arms to hug any more. She looked so pale and felt so hard and brittle. Not soft like before.

Then Dad brought her home.

"Hey, dreamer." It was one of the guys who passed us on the street. "Where're your friends?"

"How should I know? Anyway, they're not friends of mine."

"Then why're you hanging out with them?"

"Because I am. Any objections?"

"Holy crow, you're touchy."

"So why do you want to know where they are?"

"Because. Just because." Someone drops a coin in the jukebox. Elvis Presley's "Jailhouse Rock" bursts forth. "I'm Jonathon, by the way. And you are?"

"Cleopatra." My face crumples. "Sorry. I'm in a bad mood. My name's Nora. Do you go to Sutherland?"

"Yeah, grade nine."

"So how come you're talking to this jerk, Nora?" It's Dolores, grinning bright red lipstick, an unlit cigarette waving about in her right hand. I don't want to be anywhere near them.

"I'm not." I slurp the last of my Orange Crush, grab my coat and school bag. I don't even bother to say *See yah around*. I head for the door, arm half into one sleeve, the rest of the coat dangling. I can feel Dolores, Trudy, and Jonathon stare after me. Having no friends is better than hanging around with this lot.

• • •

Penticton
October 7, 1959

Dear Nora,

It was great to have a visit, even though it was short. I wish Mum didn't have to get back here so fast. Surely Dad and Gran could have looked after the boys longer. But Mum said she still has lots of canning and pickling to do and work for the church for Thanksgiving.

I wish you'd write more. We didn't even get properly caught up because I was in the hospital. I'd like to hear about the Quinns and maybe when I'm down next time I could meet them.

Mum and I talked a lot on the bus

going back. She said you remind her of Aunt Rita when they were little. I wonder if I look like Mum when she was little. I thought of asking Dad, but he didn't know her then. The only people I can ask are Aunt Alice and Auntie Beth. But we never see Aunt Alice anymore now they've moved to Montreal. And I don't remember having met Auntie Beth. Has she ever visited from California? Oh, I just thought, *Your dad would know.* He grew up with them, didn't he? But then I could ask her, too, and maybe she has some pictures. I'm going on and on.

Do you ever wonder about being our parents' age? You know, I've never thought about growing up or being grown up. Purposefully. But now, because of the operation, I do. I wonder, will you and I still be as good of friends when we're big? Maybe we'll have daughters like us. That would be nice. What would you call your daughter? I like the name Mona and also Margaret. If she was Margaret, though, I'd call her Peggy.

Did you finish *Anne of the Island*?

Mum says I'm supposed to be resting, not writing. But writing at my desk is not much different from lying in bed reading.

I'm glad we came down. You say no one at your house talks about Aunt Rita.

It's sort of the same here but different — no one here talks about my operation. But with the doctor in Vancouver I got to ask questions. Plus, I heard some of the questions Mum had. It feels more real. And more scary. I forgot to tell you that there's going to be another girl being operated on the same day. Her name is Ingrid. That's all they said. I didn't meet her.

I don't look forward to the operation but I do look forward to seeing you. And to staying at your place for the weeks after. It sounds like it may even be until Christmas. Hopefully we can do some Christmas shopping together.

Your cousin and best friend (I hope),
Lizzie

10

Thursday I have a run-in with Dad.

"Where're the pictures of Mum we used to have on the piano?"

"I put them away." Dad snaps and cracks the newspaper as he reads.

"Why?"

"Because that's where they belong," he says from behind the paper.

"I don't see why. I don't want to forget Mum." That's been bothering me for a while. "If I don't see her picture, maybe I will." Dad flicks the newspaper out straight again. It's his only comment. "There ought to be a union for kids. Someplace where we can take our complaints when parents don't listen." This gets his attention. The newspaper crackles down on his lap.

"I'm tired of your bad attitude, young lady. Go to your room and do your homework."

What bugs me is that he never used to be cross. We actually did things together. Now we never play cards or crokinole or checkers. I'm not particularly fond of crokinole because it hurts my fingers when I flick the tile, so I don't miss that. But weekends we used to play hearts and crib. If just Mum and Dad and I were there, we'd use Grandad's round cribbage board instead of the normal two-person board so that three could count easily. Now, nothing.

What do I do? Go on strike?

Go back to Penticton?

And besides, last Sunday was Thanksgiving. Jan and I cooked chicken with vegetables and made pumpkin pie for a special late lunch before she and Dot went back to St. Paul's. The meal was decent, more than decent; but no one said thank-you. No one even commented on our effort or mentioned it was Thanksgiving. Dot rattled on about her latest boyfriend. I told Jan she did a good job on the chicken. She thanked me. Other than that, we munched quietly.

Personally I am now very thankful — for all the left-overs. I am also grateful because Dad bought a TV, our first ever, and I watched *The Ed Sullivan Show*. Dad still doesn't do anything with me but at least he doesn't shove me off to bed. I guess I'm supposed to have fun with the TV instead of with him.

I want to do something with you, Dad, or
I'M GOING ON STRIKE

• • •

Today, October fifteenth, is Lizzie's birthday. I'm having my Saturday morning extra time in bed. I roll over onto my belly. Seems this is where I spend half my life. Or all of what I think of as my life. Lizzie's thirteen years old. Imagine being thirteen and maybe going to die. *You better not die, Lizzie.*

Bed is my best thinking place. The best because I think the clearest here. It's also the worst because some of what I think hurts. Anyway, right now I think of my time here with Lizzie and how selfish I was. We really had only two nights together because she spent two days in the hospital. I pretty much whined about North Vancouver the whole time and about not having a mother. Lizzie didn't say much. Is she scared?

Did you know you were dying, Mum? Were you scared? The minister says you went to Heaven and that Heaven is a good place, but how does he know?

Grandma said to me, "Don't cry, she's in a better place now." *Is that true Mum? Is it better than here? Am I going to see you when I die?* I'll be really angry if Lizzie dies. More than that. Really, really angry, because she won't have had a chance to grow up. *I try not to be angry at you, Mum. But I am sometimes. For not being here, for leaving me. Mostly, I just miss you.*

At the funeral, the air was heavy. People smiled fake sorts of smiles. Grandma's face was all pinched in but it kept smiling too. Ladies visited, people I didn't know, old people, people that felt stiff like boards and brought orange bread and tuna fish casserole. Overnight, Dad went from a happy man, someone who laughed and made stupid puns to … I'm not sure what to — a man all closed-in? My favourite thing about Dad was his laugh. Where is it now? Is Aunt Mary right? Is he struggling too? Even my bossy sister Dorothy?

March 22, 1959
Dear Nora,
  I wish you health
  I wish you wealth
  I wish you abundance and store
  I wish you Heaven after death
  What could I wish you more?
            Your former grade three teacher,
                        Mr. Weeks

Does he really believe that?
I don't believe in Heaven. Or God. How can I?

• • •

Later, I'm washing the breakfast dishes including the hated porridge pot. Jan is drying. Sort of. More like flinging the tea towel at it.

"Girls." It's Dad. His voice is in serious mode. "We have to talk about where everyone is going to sleep when Mary and Robert come down with Lizzie." Dorothy looks up from her place by our new stereo, listening to her favourite record. For the forty-three millionth time.

"Why are they coming down, Dad? They were just here." Dot lifts the needle off the record.

"For her operation." I upturn the clean porridge pot on the drying rack next to the empty milk bottles and dump the lumpy water down the sink. Jan washes off the table.

"Her operation for what?"

"Where have you been for the last century?" I sweep the porridge lumps into my hand — "For her heart, dum-mie," — and fling them in the slop pail under the sink.

"Nora, quit talking to your sister that way."

"Why can't I? That's how she talks to me, but you don't hear." I swish out the rest of the sink, dry my hands on my apron, then pull it through the handle of the refrigerator.

"Regardless, I don't want any of you talking that way. We're family. Be nice to each other."

I lean over Dot, my arms outstretched to give her a hug. She rolls her eyes at me. "Faker," I mumble.

"Careful, you." She hangs onto my hair as I pull away. Just enough so it hurts, not enough to make me squeal.

"That's better." Dad stands in the kitchen doorway. "Now back to Lizzie. They're coming down a few days before the operation."

"Can't they stay somewhere else? We don't have the room."

Dad scowls at Dot. "Aunt Mary and Uncle Robert will sleep in your room." I hear a sucked-in sort of gasp from both my sisters. "The boys are remaining behind in Penticton with Granny Frazer. Lizzie can bunk in with Nora on the camping mattress."

"What about Jan and me?" Funny how Janet doesn't say a word. Because Dorothy says enough for both of them? Or maybe she's nicer.

"I can't believe you said that, Dorothy Mackenzie." Red creeps up Dad's face. "You're here two nights out of the week, at most, and you begrudge your aunt and uncle a bed when they have to go through this? You and Jan will sleep on the floor in the rec room."

Dot turns her face to the window. "So do we at least have a mattress?"

"No, I'm thinking you might like stones or pieces of glass to sleep on. And of course no sheets or blankets."

I grin. "When are they coming exactly, Dad?"

"In two and a half weeks. Friday, November fourth, I think it is."

"For how long?" I hear Janet bang the plates down in the cupboard.

"That depends on how it goes. But we're planning for the best. Robert will go home after the operation, after they see that everything's fine. Mary'll stay on at least until Lizzie comes home from hospital. And home means here." I see Dorothy stiffen again. "Lizzie will stay with us until the doctors say she can return to Penticton. She has to be near a good hospital." I can almost see the lines of fire streak from Dad's eyes to Dot. "The success of an operation such as this — I suppose it's true of any operation but because this is such a tricky one and so new, it is doubly important — depends on having a group of highly skilled doctors and nurses and modern diagnostic aids like cardiography and a blood bank. The post-operative care must be impeccable. It's just plain lucky we're here or your aunt and uncle could not have afforded this."

I go to my room with feelings falling all over themselves. I should be happy, I know. Happy that Lizzie will be staying here and happy that Lizzie's heart will be fixed. But there'll be sickness in the house all over again.

What if it doesn't work? What then?

What if she dies?

And Mum, you were so pale and weak when you came home from hospital. There was that special bed Dad set up in the living room so you could be with us, not upstairs tucked away from all that was going on. You were so quiet, Mum. It felt like we had to whisper or it hurt you. You told me stories of when I was little. Do you remember? Like how embarrassed you were when Mrs. Boulton gave me new mitts when I was two or three and I wailed, "No fumbs, no fumbs," because she made baby mitts that are all one piece with no thumb part sticking out. And the time Vicki and I had that screaming contest until Vicki's mum phoned over and told us to be quiet. You got more of a telling off than we did.

I feel my stomach contract. It pulls and grabs at my insides. What will happen to Lizzie? She can't die. There can't be a death in this house too. There mustn't be.

> *Dear Nora,*
> > *Apple pie without cheese*
> > *Is like a kiss without a squeeze.*
> > > *Love, Uncle Robert*

11

This evening I'm tired. Very, very, very tired. Looking after the Quinns was tough. I don't know why. Their laughter seemed louder; it grated on my ears. I wanted to tell them to go jump in the lake. Or I guess the ocean is more appropriate here.

Now I'm curled up on my bed — again — with *Anne of the Island*. I read *Anne of Green Gables* three times, once with Mum and twice myself. I love *Anne* even though there are too many big words and quotations, which I don't understand and don't really want to. I remember long ago deciding when it got complicated and too full of description I'd jump over it. But Mum's eyes were like the Lake of Shining Waters when she read Anne's imaginative place names. My eyes water — again.

For Christmas last year, I got *Anne of Avonlea*. I especially like the school parts and Davy and Dora. All Davy's boldness and questions. But the first chapters of *Anne of the Island* are nowhere near as good. I had to renew it, just like Lizzie. Maybe Aunt Mary's right — it's too old for me and Lizzie. Right off I don't like the boy-girl stuff, even though I like that Anne ignores Gilbert. Some of the girls in Penticton were like that. Josie Williams, for example. This is what she wrote in my autograph book:

> *Nora now, Nora ever,*
> *Mackenzie now, But not forever.*

How dumb can you get? And Sylvia Graham's is not much better:

> *If all the boys lived across the sea,*
> *Oh what a great swimmer Nora would be.*

There are lots of things to think about other than boys, in my opinion.

In *Anne of the Island,* I particularly don't like Diana saying, "I have a feeling things will never be the same again." That's exactly how I feel, but how can Diana? Anne's only going away from home for a few months. She can come back any time she wants because Marilla is still there. Besides, she's going away with Gilbert and Charlie Sloane and will be boarding with her friend. And Diana isn't going away at all. They have no idea what it's like to go somewhere where there's no one you know, not a one. Leave everyone behind.

Including your mother.

I roll around onto my back and stare at the ceiling and out the window as usual, the book upside down on my chest. The never-ending rain drizzles down the glass and the light from the streetlamp flows in yellow waves.

But maybe Anne would understand. Her parents died, too, and she never had a real home until Avonlea. Maybe that's why home is so important to her. Like me.

The book slides off my chest as I tuck my hands underneath my head and stare around the room, at the blackboard, my old brown bureau, the closet, and the white desk Uncle Robert made for me, the exact same as Lizzie's.

Maybe I'll never go back to Penticton. Maybe that's what Anne means by a "bend in the road." I've gone around a bend and can never go back. Maybe Dad will never be happy, maybe Dot will always be silly and boy-crazy and hate me. But I do like the Quinns. Maybe I have to choose a way to be happy. Or a place.

Oh, Mum, I'm all muddled up.

I've cried so much you'd think my crying glands would have dried up by now. But I feel wet streaks on my cheeks. They match the rain on the windowpane.

And Anne's favourite person, her kindred spirit, Matthew, died too. Why do people have to die?

• • •

I wake, fully clothed, to the light shining from my bedside lamp. I twist the switch to off. Blackness engulfs me as I crawl under the covers. My blackboard still reads:

TALK TO ME
DAD
TALK TO ME
ABOUT MUM

• • •

Monday, Mrs. Bramley announces in Music class the school's going to put on *The Wizard of Oz*. I sang in the Junior and Intermediate church choirs in Penticton but I haven't sung at all since before Mum got sick. Even around the house. I don't know why. It doesn't feel right. I check "choir" anyway on the list at the back of the room and I almost agree I'd do costumes, too, but change my mind.

Tuesday at four, straight after announcements, I head for room 9A. I'm third there and find a desk by the window. With Mrs. Bramley on the autoharp, we stumble through "We're Off to See the Wizard" and "Ding-Dong the Witch is Dead" about ten times each until I have them nearly all memorized. I wait until the others straggle out. The room's empty, except for Trudy.

"What're you doing here?"

"The same thing as you, I guess." I am definitely not happy to see her. Part of the reason for coming to practices is to be away from her and Dolores.

"You like singing?"

"Uh-huh. I used to be in a choir in Penticton."

"Me too. Not Penticton. But Prince George. In the school choir."

"Where's Dolores?"

"Does it matter?"

"I thought you were her best friend."

"Only friend. Maybe not even that."

"Still, where's Dolores?"

"Look, I'd rather stay away from her."

"How come?"

"She does mean things. But mainly I don't like going to her house. It's funny there."

"Funny ha ha or funny peculiar?"

"Funny peculiar. It gives me the creeps. Don't go there."

"I don't even know where she lives." *Not really, anyway.*

"Well, if you want my advice, keep it that way." I hold the school door open for Trudy.

"Have you put your name down for a special role?"

"Nah, I don't think I could." We walk down the corridor together. It feels awkward. "Did you see that Jinx was at rehearsal too?"

"Jinx? Who's Jinx?"

"You know, Jonathon. The guy at the café. That's his nickname." We cross over Grand Boulevard in silence.

"Got to turn here." I give her a half wave. "See you Thursday."

• • •

The next day after school I just get in the front door when the back doorbell rings. It's Stella with a smile on her face.

"Come see the kittens."

I hop over the picket fence, barely missing the rhubarb. There on the porch, in the quilt-padded cardboard box, are four, mostly black, tiny rat-like creatures, two curled up asleep, the other two nursing. Carmody — in other words Fluffy — purrs contentedly.

"Can we pick them up, Mrs. Taylor?"

"Of course, dear. Fluffy will tell you if she doesn't want you to." Mrs. Taylor seems softer today. Maybe she likes kittens too. I wonder if she wanted babies of her own.

I slip my hands under each kitten in turn, stroke their soft fur and explore their markings. One has white fur around his eye with black everywhere else, another has white boots only. A third is all black. They have cords dangling from their bellies. When I lift up the fourth, I know immediately she's my favourite. She's smaller than the others — teeny, teeny — and has a touch of white under her chin.

"When do they open their eyes?" Stella asks her aunt.

"I don't know. Let's wait and see."

The small warm creature wriggles in my hand and mews, her head moving, searching.

"She's looking for her mother, for food."

I slide her in next to Carmody. The kitten immediately sucks away at her mum's little nipple. Carmody licks the tiny body. It looks so peaceful. And comforting. "I wish I could keep her, Mrs. Taylor."

"If your dad says you can have a kitten, you can pick whichever one you like."

"Really? Oh thanks, Mrs. Taylor. I'll call her Juniper."

"Me too, Aunt Grace?"

"That depends on what your mother says."

• • •

In Thursday's practice I sit next to Ava. Alvina is home sick with a cold. I see Jonathon and Trudy sitting beside each other. I try to smile. My Mackenzie gran always says, "Don't forget to turn the sides of your mouth up." Honestly, lately I have tried. But it doesn't seem to help much in the friendship department here.

• • •

Dear Nora,
> *Three little rules we all should keep*
> *To make life happy and bright*
> *Smile in the morning, smile at noon*
> *And keep on smiling at night.*
>> *Sincerely, Mrs. Jenkins*

Honestly, I have tried Mrs. Jenkins.

• • •

Saturday, I take the children to the park for about an hour until raindrops-that-threaten-to-be-a-downpour start. The rest of the afternoon we read *The Wizard of Oz*. I got the book out of the library. When the kids get wiggly I teach them songs.

"Mrs. Quinn, my cousin's coming down, not this Friday, but next, for an operation. Can she come babysitting with me here on Saturday? That is, if she is up to it."

"How old is she?"

"She turned thirteen last week."

"Well, I'm quite sure it'll be fine. As long as you remember you're the one responsible for the children. What kind of operation is she having?"

"I don't know what it's called, but they're fixing a hole in her heart."

"That's really serious." I can see the colour drain from Mrs. Quinn's face. "I'm glad to hear they can do an operation for it now. I knew a small boy who died because of a hole in his heart." Her body straightens. "I didn't tell you about our Beatrice, did I?" I can feel something coming. "She had polio. She was late getting the inoculation because we were living in northern Alberta at the time." Mrs. Quinn takes a deep breath. Her face returns to its normal colour. "I look forward to meeting your cousin. What did you say her name was?"

•••

Penticton, B.C., Canada
The World, The Solar System
The Universe
October 18, 1959

Dear Nora,
Thanks for the letter. "At last," I said when it came. And thanks for the gorgeous birthday card you made. I counted the candles the first time and got fourteen. "Whoops," I said to myself. But it was me, not you. There were definitely thirteen. We had a little party. Mum made the usual cake with a matchstick, button, and thimble, as well as a penny, dime, and a quarter wrapped in waxed paper and baked inside. Jack and Dougie got the penny and dime. I got the quarter. I think Mum must somehow mark the cake so she knows where to cut so we each get something good. On my second piece of cake (yes, yes I was a little piggy) I got the

thimble. That means I'll never marry.

Dad gave me a diary to write in while I am in hospital and Mum made me a pretty nightie for the hospital too. The boys went together (with Mum's help obviously) and got me a book about animals and birds. They said it was for when I was in Vancouver, but I think really it's so I can teach them that stuff later. I guess that's a mean thing to say. It was a good day.

When I came home to your place from the hospital last month, I didn't want to talk about it or think about it. The hospital, I mean. Now that's all I want to do. Do you mind if I tell you? You can skip this part if you want.

It was only two days, but I hated the poking and prodding, the blood work and the X-rays, first one nurse then another, one doctor, then another. I felt like a slab of meat being thrown around. Sometimes I wondered if any of them even knew I had a name. But the worst part was, not because it was painful but because it was embarrassing, they stuck a tube down my throat to look at my heart (That's what I thought they said, but how can they see my heart through my throat?). Afterwards I threw up all over myself and the bed. Egads.

I liked our time together in North Vancouver. I know you miss Penticton and everyone, and of course your mum, but I think you're lucky to have your dad and sisters close by. Just imagine if you were in Penticton, you wouldn't have Jan and Dorothy, except at Christmas probably. And you've got the Quinns. It's like they're your family, too, but you get paid to look after them. I'm always looking after Jack and Dougie and never get paid.

On the bus coming back, I told Mum I was scared about the operation not working. She said a part of her was scared, too, but really she knew it would be fine. I asked her how she knew, and she said, "Because it has to be. Because I keep saying it will be fine and you (meaning me) have to think that way too. You will grow up and be my Lizzie long after I die." I could feel the tears coming up into my eyes. I can feel my throat squeeze in even now.

Then the conversation went like this: "Oh, Mum. Don't say that. You'll never die."

"Oh, dear. It feels like that and I want to stay around as long as possible."

"Just don't die on me like Auntie Rita, I couldn't stand that."

"Then, you don't die on me either. You come through that operation with flying colours. Do we have a deal?"

I remember saying, "It's a deal." But Nor, I'm still scared. It may sound crazy, but for a while I was cross that no one asked if I wanted this operation or not. I didn't have the nerve to say anything. But I know I do want it for sure. For absolutely for sure. But I wished someone had asked. I'm sick and tired of sitting on the sidelines of my life. I always watch. I give out bibs in field hockey. I read at the beach. If this operation works, I can have a life. It's my one chance for a big life. And I'm taking it.

Gotta run. Maybe I should start using my new diary for writing all this stuff instead of my letters to you. Sorry. But I did warn you.

Lizzie

PS See you soon and thanks again for the card.

Sunday morning I wake to a sweet fragrance wafting from the kitchen and scramble into my around-the-house clothes. No church clothes here like in Penticton. Dad never goes to church now and doesn't insist that us girls go either. That's okay because I don't think I believe in God or church or Heaven anymore.

"Bran muffins for breakfast straight from the oven." Janet scrapes around the sides of each muffin with a knife and flicks them up to cool.

"So how come you're being so nice?"

"Is that the thanks I get for all this work, and on my day off?" Janet whacks me gently on the head with her oven mitts. I pick out a muffin that sits at a jaunty angle in the muffin pan.

"Thanks, Jan and ... *mmmm* ... you put dates in them. My favourite." I take a crumbly bite and drop it back out onto a plate, waving away the heat from my mouth. "Yikes, they're scalding hot."

"I told you they were straight out of the oven."

"Can you show me how to make them, Jan? Maybe Mrs. Quinn would let me and kids make some too."

Janet hands me a stained three-inch by five-inch card. "Here's Mum's recipe. It's really clear. Take it. But make sure you ask Mrs. Quinn first."

I grab a small plate for under my mouth to catch the crumbs. "I'll copy it."

At the top of a new recipe card I print _Rita Mackenzie's Date and Bran Muffins_, adding curly tails to the capital letters to make them look fancy. "So I put the flour and baking soda in one bowl and the hot water and dates in another?"

"Yeah, do the dates first. And make sure you cut them really small so you don't miss a pit. You don't want any broken teeth."

"And the egg and milk go in another bowl. Then you pour the dates and the milk mixture all into the flour and stuff, right?"

"Yup. Pour it all in at one time and mix, just enough to get all the dry ingredients wet." Janet bends over the table. "See, Mum wrote ..."

"Jan, does it hurt to see Mum's handwriting on the card?"

"Oh, Norrie, of course it does."

"Then why don't you tell me?" My words sound lumpy and weird. Not muffin lumpy. "I thought it was just me."

"Because it hurts too much. It's easier to be bossy and mean." She gives my head a stroke

"You're bossy, but not mean like Dot. Can you teach me to cook? How can I learn without Mum around?"

"Sure, kiddliwinks. It's a deal. But Dad says you already cook great meals."

"Stew, stew, and stew. Oh and a pathetic spaghetti sauce. I want to learn how to make fancy cookies and cakes. Maybe even pies."

"That's more than a start. We'll do some simple baked things together. You've got lots of years to learn all the rest."

I continue to write, humming "We're Off to See the Wizard." Jan doesn't seem to mind. She rattles the dishes in the sink as I copy.

"Where's Dot? Still in bed?"

"I guess. Would you like me to play that on the piano? We have the sheet music." Janet digs in the piano bench.

"We'll wake Dot."

"So? Ah, here it is." Janet drops the lid and plops down on the bench. I slip in beside her. Just like old times. Only it used to be Mum playing. We'd sing from our tattered red *Canada Sings* book: "Old Lang Syne," "I'll Take You Home Again, Kathleen," "O My Darling Clementine."

"I'd like to be able to play like you, Jan. And Mum. Can you teach me that too?"

"Get Dad to find you a real teacher. A good teacher, kiddliwinks. I wouldn't know how, and anyway, I'm your sister. Remember, I'm bossy. I'd be too bossy about your practising."

She gives me a sideways hug. It's been such a long time since I've had hugs from her, in our non-huggy family. Good, genuine hugs.

We sing and sing — from *The Wizard of Oz, My Fair Lady, The King and I*. In a while, even Dad joins us in his lush tenor, mug of instant coffee in one hand and muffin in the other. "The Red River Valley," "Cockles and Mussels," "Annie Laurie."

"I really got a kick out of that, girls." Dad puts his coffee down as if to leave. "Thanks. That's the nicest time I've had in many moons." Dad talks in a lumpy sort of way — with his mouth full of a second (or is it a third?) muffin. "These are great, Jan."

"Not so great for me. You guys woke me up." Dorothy stomps up the stairs, sleepy-eyed in her crinkled flannelette pyjamas and mussed-up hair. "You could at least have waited until I was up."

"Any decent person should be awake by nine a.m." I think it, but Jan says it.

"I smell muffins." She turns to the kitchen.

"Sorry, there're all eaten." It's Dad. I can't believe he said that.

"You mean and nasty people. And thoughtless. And greedy."

He laughs. "And someone sure is gullible. Do you think we could eat a whole dozen muffins between us?" He nudges Dorothy towards the kitchen. "And your whining will not spoil the nice time I've just had. Go get your breakfast. And thank your sister Jan for the fresh baking."

Dorothy scowls. Janet pokes me in the ribs with her elbows.

• • •

After supper, there's a knock on my bedroom door. I like it closed. It's my space, especially when Jan and Dot are home. But they've gone back to the hospital and now I've finished my homework. Dad plops down on the bed.

"I've seen it, Nora. It's just hard." For a moment I don't know what he's talking about. He nods towards the blackboard — the talk-to-me-about-Mum stuff. "But today, all that singing makes it easier for some reason."

"Why is it hard, Dad?"

"Lots of reasons. I miss your mother very much. I miss her for you girls too. I'm not good at being both dad and mum to you. But mostly because I should have been able to save her. Or, at least I should have known earlier she was so sick."

"That doesn't help me, Dad. Now." I swivel around. The chair legs scrape on the floor.

"You're right. Guess I'm being selfish."

"You're not selfish, Dad." I want to reach forward and give him a hug but don't. The non-huggy-type family again. "Maybe you're unhappy like me."

"You're a wise young woman." I don't think I've ever seen his face squinchy before.

"Not really. Aunt Mary reminded me, that's all." He reaches out and pats my knee.

"That singing was wonderful. When I first heard it this morning, I was back with Rita. Do you know that's how I met your mother?"

"I thought you grew up together."

"Yes and no. We both grew up just up the road from Penticton, in Summerland. It was even smaller than it is now but our family went to the downtown church, the Gladwins went to the uptown church."

I uncurl my legs and watch Dad as he runs his hands through the waves of his hair. He has a little grey at the temples now too. The sadness is gone. His large blue eyes are smiley, remembering.

"We both were in *The Mikado*. You know, the Gilbert and Sullivan operetta. Back then, before the war, the Singers and Players put on a Gilbert and Sullivan piece every year. I played Nanki-Poo."

"I knew you had a good voice, but not that good."

"Actually, I was not bad." He starts humming "A Wand'ring Minstrel, I." "Mostly it was great fun." Dad chuckles. It's so good to hear him laugh. And sing too. "Your mother was in the chorus. She was the prettiest girl in the whole place. Funny how I'd never seen her in Summerland before — but I was two years ahead of her in school and I worked in the cannery down by the lake. She lived out by Giant's Head. Our lives were much narrower then — our social life was church and work and school. If it wasn't the same church or work or grade at school, you didn't meet."

I don't interrupt. I can't ever remember a time when my dad told stories like this. We played games, sure, but he never was a storyteller, never talked about the past.

"I was in medicine at the Vancouver General. But early in the fall I got sick from drinking water from a flume. You remember, we irrigated the fruit trees by running water through flumes back then. Anyway, I was off sick for about two months. I had lost too much time to go back to medical school so I worked the rest of the year at the cannery. That winter we had such a merry time in the Singers and Players. The next year, I went back into medicine. I went out with lots of girls in Vancouver, but when your mother came back from nursing training in Alberta, I had eyes for no one but her." The talking makes Mum more real again, even her face and voice are clear to me.

"Did Mum really have cancer?"

"Acute leukemia. That's cancer of the blood. It gets bad very fast."

The feeling in the room changes, the warm mood of before is gone. The gentleness in his eyes has altered to ... I'm not sure what. Anger? Regret? Sadness?

"That's what Aunt Mary said, but I still don't see why you had to change jobs, why we had to leave Penticton." I think out loud.

"Maybe we didn't. Maybe we should have stayed. But then we wouldn't see Dorothy and Janet so often. It's hard enough for me to lose your mother, without having two of my daughters move away almost at the same time. Plus, we wouldn't have had this fun today. And then we wouldn't be here for Aunt Mary and Uncle Robert." He takes a deep breath. A cheery, I-must-be-cheery, sort of breath.

"Dad, I was wondering if I could have piano lessons. Janet and Dot got them. I didn't."

"We'll see." That means *no*.

"But I'd really like to play like Mum."

"I said, we'll see." He pats me on the shoulder and rises. He's clearly had enough of our talking. I don't like his non-answer about lessons but I figure I can always look for a piano teacher myself. Maybe Mrs. Bramley will know.

• • •

I'm almost halfway through *Anne of the Island*. Now I realize why Lizzie didn't finish it. Ruby, one of the Anne's friends, is dying. Of "galloping consumption" it says. My

Highroads Dictionary says that's tuberculosis. I assume the galloping part means it's getting worse fast, galloping along like a horse. Whatever, it doesn't matter. Ruby is dying. Not that I like the character Ruby. What I really don't like is that everybody seems to know she's dying except Ruby and her family. Was it the same with me? Did everyone at school, everyone at church in Penticton *know* that my mother was going to die?

What about Lizzie? Do all the kids at Pen High think she's going to die? Are Aunt Mary and Uncle Robert and even my dad pretending too? Despite what they say?

• • •

> *To my favourite little sister, Nora—*
> *Love many*
> *Trust few*
> *Always paddle your own canoe.*
> *July 3/59*
> *Janet L. Mackenzie*

I wonder why Jan wrote that? Does she wonder who she can trust?

Why do people have to die?

Who can I trust to tell me the truth?

Can I trust myself?

13

At 6:45 I arrive on the Quinns' doorstep. This is the first time I get a chance to babysit during the week. Dad was reluctant, but Mrs. Quinn said it was for only two hours.

"Thanks, dear. You're a life saver. The meeting should be over by eight-thirty, and I'll be back as soon as I can after that." She slips her arms into her coat.

"Glad I can help, Mrs. Quinn."

"Oh," she pauses with the door half closed behind her. "Maureen and Patricia want a bath. But they have to be in bed by eight. Colin hates baths so don't worry about him. He's normally in bed earlier — seven-thirty or so. Just do your best." And off she goes into the dark night.

The bathroom door is open and the room all lit up. Maureen kneels on the counter, twisting her hair into skinny corkscrew wisps and trying to touch the end of her tongue to her nose. She laughs at her faces in the mirror. Patricia sits on the toilet with the lid down, reddy-golden curls tumbling over the shoulders of her green dressing gown. Colin runs his metal truck up and down the tile lines on the floor and wall with a *vroom vroom* to match the crackle and bounce of the tires. He's already in his pyjamas.

"Oh, hi, Nor. Can we turn the tap on now?"

Through the mist of steam the girls strip down and tuck their toes into the water. I run to the kitchen for two plastic bowls. They dip and dump them over each other, squealing with delight. Colin and I seem to get as much water on us as they do.

"Can I go in too?" Colin's already peeling off his bottoms.

"No. You hate baths." Patricia stretches her legs out straight to take up as much space in the tub as possible.

"No, I don't." Colin's pyjama top lands in the sink, as he scrambles in between the two girls. He bends and slops water over his head too.

"Your mum said you didn't like baths."

"Mum scrubs us like we're dirty parsnips. That's what she calls us." Colin throws a load of water at me. "And I hate parsnips." I jump sideways. He laughs.

"Oh no you don't, young man." I dump a wriggling wet body on the squishy bathmat. "Now wrap up in this towel and sit." The word *sit* comes out hard and firm, like I'm training a puppy. I guess I am.

Colin's room has a mattress under the window with a dresser beside it. The walls are plastered with pictures of animals: elephants, tigers, bears, crocodiles, kangaroos, wolves, and monkeys. I find pyjamas rolled up in the bottom drawer. Sighing, I tuck three library books under my arm and trot back towards the noise. This is not easy babysitting. Patricia's fingers massage a frothy mass of golden curls. Maureen's eyes squeeze shut, soap drizzles over her cheeks and drips off her chin.

"I'll help you girls with the rinsing. But let me sort Colin out first." I swivel around. Where's Colin? A small naked boy stands in the sink, a tall, ice-blue bottle in hand, drinking.

I grab the bottle and sweep Colin up in a towel. White gloppy stuff rolls down over his belly. How much has he drunk? I run to the phone. *Answer quick, Dad. Please. Please.*

"It's Colin, Dad. He's drunk something. Come quick. I don't want him to die."

• • •

Three minutes seem like three hours. I wait at the door, Colin on a chair beside me, wrapped up in a big blue towel. Not a word out of him.

"Well, young man. What have you been drinking instead of playing in the bath?" Dad-in-doctor-mode says to Colin when he arrives.

"This stuff. It's yummy." Colin points to the almost empty bottle in my hand.

"Milk of Magnesia." I read from the label.

Patricia and Maureen in dressing gowns, towels draped over their heads, watch from the stairs

"Ooof. How can you say that's yummy? It's horrid." Maureen nods at her sister.

Dad kneels down to Colin. "How much did you drink, son?"

"Lots and lots." Colin says with a grin.

"It was about half full, Mr. Mackenzie." Patricia looks paler than usual. It's not that she's extra clean, I realize. "Mum takes it every once in a while."

"There was lots on his stomach, Dad." I open the towel. "See." There's a chalky layer over Colin's belly and the inside of the towel.

"Milk of Magnesia is for when you find it hard to go to the bathroom." He pats Colin's head. "I think the most you'll have, young man, is a stomach ache and the trots."

"Yuck."

"*Ooooh*, my stomach is sore. Really sore." Colin curls down over his legs, a broad smile on his face.

My knees feel weak.

Dad collects Colin into his arms and seeks out the living room. "How about if I read to you, son."

• • •

There's a quiet in the house. I can hear Dad's words, a low rumble from downstairs.

"Will you read to us, please, Nora?" Patricia and Maureen linger in the doorway, subdued, hair partly dried and brushed. My body aches from the strain. From the worry, I guess, too. I empty the water in the tub and mop the wet from the linoleum floor with the bathmat.

"Do your teeth first, girls. Then call me when you're settled in bed."

I wipe out the tub, hang the soaked bathmat over the side, and fold the towels over the shower curtain pole to dry.

When I finally head downstairs, Colin's asleep on Dad's lap.

• • •

Dear Nora,
> *Nora, Nora in the tub*
> *Mother forgot to put in the plug*
> *Oh my heart, oh my soul,*
> *There goes Nora down the hole.*

> *Jenny*

• • •

I've been going over to the Taylors' mostly every day after school to see the kittens. Each time I'm amazed by the change in them. I can almost see them grow. Stella hasn't been there in a while, but today she is, wearing a warm woollen coat. The weather feels like winter even though it's still October. Mrs. Taylor has brought the kitten-filled cat bed into the screened-in porch.

"Look, Nora, those dangly bits have fallen off."

"Yah, they did last week."

"What're they for."

"They're called umbilical cords. The babies are attached to their mother that way inside her stomach. You were too." Stella's eyes open.

"How do you know this stuff?"

"Because my dad's a doctor. Plus I have two big sisters who tell me things." Having my dad a doctor is definitely useful. "Their eyes have started to open too." The kittens wiggle and worm their way around, nuzzle each other and their mum, making tiny mewing sounds.

• • •

October 24, 1959
(eleven days until I see you again)

Dear Nora,

Jack has a bad cold. That means I have to be in bed too and take penicillin. That's always how we've done it from a way back. In order that I stay well, if one of us is sick, we all have to take medicine, and I have to stay home from school along with the sick one. I think we take more medicine in this family than all the people of Penticton together. That's an exaggeration, obviously, but it feels like it. I told Mum it was probably healthier to be at school than at home with Jack's drippy nose and snuffles and whines. But oh no. Mum says, "Your Uncle Alan says so and that's what we do." I blame your dad for this one.

After I whined and whined like Jack, she looked at me with that awful stare she sometimes has and said, "We can't afford for you to get sick at this time. You need that operation." She doesn't have to say more — her face says it for her.

Anyway, it means I get to lie around and write to you and finish off my Christmas presents for everyone. I've knitted a scarf for Dad, and toques for the boys (I made them to fit me, so if they don't fit now they'll grow into them).

By the way, thanks for the letter. It was "fantabulous, grandificient, marveltastic," to quote you. I hope you get an answer for your piano teacher advertisement. Remember how fast you heard back from Mrs. Quinn?

Why didn't you try out for an individual part in *The Wizard of Oz*? Isn't there a good witch or something? Or you could have been the Cowardly Lion, who's brave underneath, because, even though you don't think so, you are enormously brave to move and go to a new school.

My teachers are giving me homework and more homework while I'm away in Vancouver. Maybe we can do it together when I get out of hospital?

Must go. I promised Mum I'd heat up the soup for her. Funny how I don't have to be in bed when it suits her!

See you soon.

Just call me Cowardly Lion, number 2.

Lizzie

14

It's Friday, the fourth of November. Lizzie's coming. I rush home after school to bring in the laundry. Despite the clouds, everything has blown dry in the wind. The full washing line squeaks and squeals as I yank it in, arm over arm. First, I roll up Dad's socks in pairs, after relieving them of their sock stretchers. I toss his long pants, my blouses, the tea towels, and handkerchiefs into the basket for ironing later. Then the towels and pillow cases. The sheets, what I need most, are the last of course.

I breathe in the wonderful smell of freshness and outdoors as I make up my mattress on the floor. Lizzie has my bed. It reminds me of when we used to sleep out in our tent in the backyard in Penticton. I scrawl a new message on my blackboard.

WELCOME

LIZZIE

WELCOME

Dad has put a roast in the oven. I peel carrots and potatoes and add them around the pot. Then I put an extra leaf in the Arborite table and set it for seven — placemats, serviettes and large plates, knives, forks, and spoons. Salt and pepper in the middle. I search the garden for flowers — Mum always had them on the table — but there are only a few droopy chrysanthemums that desperately need throwing away. I check the front steps. Yes. The milkman has brought the extra bottles we ordered.

Six o'clock and Janet and Dorothy blow in as usual. The clouds have settled in with a solid rain.

"If it's raining southeast of here, they'll have had to take it slowly," Dad says when I start to chew my nails. "There might even be snow on Allison Pass." I iron the blouses, tea towels, and hankies without being asked — to keep my mind off worrying.

• • •

Dear Nora,
    I saw you in the ocean
    I saw you in the sea
    I saw you in the bathtub
    Oops, excuse me.
        Yours 'til the kitchen sinks, Brian

Dear Nora,
    Starkle starkle little twink
    I wonder why you are I think
    Bet you wish you could be me

Starkle starkle little twink.
Your pal, Steven

Honestly, guys write the stupidest things.

• • •

It's ten to seven. I hear the car turn into the gravel drive and run to the door. In front of the others, Lizzie puffs and pants up the stairs. Her black curly hair bounces. She smiles. But the smile that used to be broad, lighting up her whole face, is only with her eyes now. And the light shining through those deep blue eyes is even less than a few weeks ago.

"The snow was quite heavy in the Pass with those big, fluffy, spattery flakes on the windshield," explains Uncle Robert. "As we came down into the valley it turned to ice rain and then rain. It was not fun."

"And the traffic. I don't know how people cope with it all the time." Aunt Mary sighs a tired sigh. "But something sure smells delicious." She smiles at me and brightens. "Nora. Turn around. Let me see." I obey. "Hey, you've really got the hang of that French braid now. Good for you." I beam back. It's nice someone notices.

"You and Robert, go put your feet up for a few minutes before supper," says Dad. "We'll call you when the vegetables are done. Jan and Dot can put the finishing touches on the meal."

"Which one's your suitcase, Lizzie?" I ask. Uncle Robert points and I grab the red one.

• • •

After supper we head straight for bed. That is, Lizzie and me. That sounds corny. Sort of like we're going to sleep at 7:45. We're not. We have so much to talk about and it's easier cuddled up in bed under layers of blankets. We talk about school, friends, and more school, and we end with our usual game of ... well, we don't have a name for it. Dirt — earth — sky — blue — bird — fly — mosquito — bee — honey — toast — breakfast — eggs — bacon — pig — spider — ("Where did you get spider from pig?" asks Lizzie. "Oh, I get it, *Charlotte's Web*.") — web ... and as always one of us drifts off. This time it's Lizzie.

I'm left thinking. But not for long.

• • •

Saturday morning I crawl into Lizzie's bed — my bed but hers now — and tell her about Juniper and the other kittens. I'm just about to say I hope I can have one, when a whiff of something wonderfully wonderful slips in and invades the room.

"Aah, I know what that smell is," says Lizzie. "We brought down a box of Newtown apples for you. I bet that's Mum making her special applesauce to go with her usual at-home Saturday morning pancakes."

I throw my dressing gown on and run to the kitchen. "Oh, you don't know how good it is to have you here." *Almost as good as having Mum*, I say to myself. I fling my arms around her middle.

"Good morning, my dear. Sit yourself down and tell me about school these days." Aunt Mary extracts herself from my hug and lifts the first lot of pancakes onto a plate in the warming oven. "Do you like it any better?"

"Well, *The Wizard of Oz* is good. But the rest is about the same. In Social Studies I sit near the window and stare outside most of the time. I can't remember which kings of England are which and who is on what side of what in all their wars."

"Yeah, me too. I almost fall asleep." Lizzie joins us in her yellow cotton nightie.

"Go put on your dressing gown, love." Lizzie screws up her face but disappears back into the bedroom.

"Sometimes I think I'll actually nod off and the teacher will find me snoring with my chin in my hands."

Aunt Mary laughs. "Is it that bad, girls?" She flips the next three pancakes as Lizzie comes back into the kitchen and drags out another chair. "Don't they make it more exciting than when I was your age?"

"You got that stuff too?"

"Sure mike. I could never remember where York was in England and why it was important compared to London. I don't understand why they don't give you the history of Canada or B.C. The early trail for the gold rush to the Klondike came right through Penticton for heaven's sake. Now that's exciting." She places the second load of pancakes on the plate in the warming oven.

"Maybe they don't think gold rushes and Indians and building railroads are as important as kings and queens and wars."

"True, but there were wars here too." She drizzles more

batter into the cast iron frying pan. "I guess they see their wars as more important than our wars."

"Anyway, why should history be about wars? Why not about people and what they did to get along with each other?"

"Now that sounds like the words of a wise young woman." Aunt Mary gives Lizzie a hug. *Or the history of the development of heart surgery*, I think but don't say because I don't want to break the happy mood. "Nora, run and tell everyone breakfast will be in two minutes."

. . .

At 12:45 we arrive at the Quinns' doorstep. Lizzie finds the walk hard, even though half of it is downhill. Her lungs wheeze. We stop a lot. The afternoon goes quickly and easily, however. It fines-up so we play in the back garden. But when Mrs. Quinn returns she sits us down.

"You may not want to hear this, but there is something I have to say." She turns to Lizzie. "I know you're going to have a serious operation in a couple of days. I'm also sure Nora told you about Beatrice, that she died of polio. My lovely girl who would be a year older than you girls now." She pauses. A shadow crosses her face.

My mental brakes scream: *Stop. Stop. Stop.* I don't want to hear this. I wish adults would keep their mouths shut. We don't need whatever she's about to say. What's Mrs. Quinn up to?

"This might sound like a sermon, but here it is." She barely takes a breath. Lizzie and I don't have time to interrupt or make an excuse about going. "Both of you have had hard lives. You, Nora, because your mother died. You,

Lizzie, because you've had to live with a body that has threatened to give out on you since you were little."

I see Lizzie squirm. Is she thinking like me? Here we go again. Another adult telling us what it's like or how we should be.

"I remember my Bea when she got ill. Very quickly she went from having her legs not work to being in an iron lung. All she could do was lie there. Some children got better. Others didn't. She was one of the unlucky ones. We couldn't even hug her. What I found the hardest though, after losing Bea, was other people. It was like they didn't want to talk about it."

My head pounds. I like Mrs. Quinn. Why must she talk about dying? Can't she leave us alone? Does she think Lizzie is going to die? I feel my arms push on my legs as if to get me out of here but they don't move.

"For a long time I chose to ignore what happened. The polio. Her dying. I thought I did something wrong to bring the polio on her, that it was my fault."

I glance at Lizzie. She's staring at the floor. I wonder if Aunt Mary also thinks she did something wrong to give Lizzie a hole in her heart.

"What I want to say is, if it's like that for you, if you're worried about things or you want to talk, do. Talk about it. Take off the mask of pretend that everything's fine."

I feel my shoulders lift. That's it? The mask of pretend? *You should talk to Dad*, my head says. I want to get out of here, fast. For me. For Lizzie. The silence fills up with our breathing. I don't know what to say. I have no words. I should not have brought Lizzie here. Mrs. Quinn peers out the backdoor window.

"Looks like Colin needs rescuing from his big sisters." She pauses as she heads for the door. "And Lizzie. Best of luck, and remember there are lots of us sitting on those doctors' shoulders — very gently of course — making sure the operation goes right."

Lizzie's smile is weak.

• • •

We walk back slowly in silence, except for Lizzie's heavy breathing. The afternoon had been fun. We'd played dress-up at first, read stories, turned the skipping rope for the girls while Colin played in the damp sand pile. And then this *whammo* with Mrs. Quinn.

"No wonder you like Mrs. Quinn."

My head doesn't know how or where to stop spinning. Lizzie's okay with it? "We've never talked about any of this before."

"But she's right. I do wear a mask. Sometimes I've felt like giving up. Then I would consciously say, *This is my life*. My life's different, a sitting-on-the-sidelines-sort-of-life. But that's the way it is and it's all mine."

"Oh, Lizzie." I squeeze her hand. "You told me that in a letter. Why didn't you tell me before?"

"I don't know. I guess I thought you wouldn't under-stand." She plunks down on the low wall bordering the sidewalk, her chest heaving.

"You're right. Maybe before I wouldn't have."

"And now, Tuesday. I've been waiting for this day for as long as I can remember, hoping doctors would find a way to make me better without cutting me open. But I really always knew I was headed for this operation, whether I wanted it or not. Come what may. Like other girls knowing they'll grow up to be a teacher. But no one actually said it." She pushes herself to standing. We turn the corner on Ridgeway. "Really I want it all to go away."

"Yeah. But don't forget what you said in your letter. You're getting a big chance at a big life." I squeeze her hand tight.

A shadow hovers beneath a young copper beech tree, its leaves still hanging on reddish in the late autumn evening. I stop. The shadow breaks into two. Two crouching girls.

"Dolores? Stella?"

"Hi, Nora," says Stella in a small voice.

"What are you two doing here?" I barely recognize Dolores. Instead of the usual sweater set, swirly skirt, and makeup, she has on old baggy pants, no eyeliner or mascara, and definitely no red lipstick or kiss curls or cigarette.

"Nothing." Dolores answers in a way that clearly says, "Leave us alone, don't talk to us."

"What do you mean nothing? You look like two frightened rabbits."

"We've run away from home."

"Shush, Stella. How do you know Nora?" By the yellowish streetlight, the little girl's face shows stains of tears.

"She's the one that lives next to Aunt Irene's. Remember, I told you about her and the kittens."

The penny drops. "You mean you're sisters?" Of course, I realize. Her big sister, Lori. Dolores. Why am I blown away? Because Stella is so nice and cute and sweet, and Dolores is, well, not? "This is my cousin Lizzie. She's from the Okanagan." Lizzie leans against the tree.

"Oh, I've never been there." Stella uncurls. She looks smaller than I remember. And tired. "Is it nice?"

"I think so." Lizzie smiles.

"Well, we gotta go." Dolores again with that don't-ask-any-more-questions voice.

"Us too. I thought you're running away from home, though. Are you sure you're all right?"

Dolores punches Stella's shoulder. The little girl winces. "Ouch. Don't do that."

"Of course we're all right."

"See you Monday, then. And Dolores, don't hit her. She's a nice kid. And my friend."

15

Monday morning, just before I leave for school, Lizzie crawls into the back of their wine-coloured Austin, off to the hospital. Off to her operation. Will I ever see her again alive? I swallow hard. Are the others thinking the same? But their faces are all smiles. Their masks. I hear the mournful *whooo-hooo* of a foghorn. Over and over. Over and over. Lizzie unrolls the window.

"Hey, Nora. That foghorn. That's a descending fourth. Remember that when you start learning the piano." She says it loud enough for Dad to hear — Lizzie's way of reminding him I want to play. I still haven't had a response from my advertisement at the library and I keep forgetting to ask Mrs. Bramley.

Uncle Robert gets into the driver's seat of course, with Aunt Mary next to him. I watch her crane her neck at the snow-glazed mountains above the foggy harbour as the car disappears into the gloom. Will I ever get used to the fog and the rain?

• • •

In Science class Dolores is missing. She's really good in Science. You wouldn't think it because she doesn't answer in class or show off. At the beginning of the year she was nearly always top of the class on the quizzes. According to Trudy, her father worked on the bridge that fell down and he has heaps of science books at home. Maybe Dolores reads them for fun. But lately her marks have dropped.

• • •

February 27, 1959
My Dearest Nora,
    Good better best,
    Never let it rest
    Till your good is better
    and your better best.
                Love, Dad

• • •

After school I check in on the kittens. Like Dolores, Stella's not there either. Juniper is still my favourite. She walks in a wobbly sort of way, falling over herself and her brothers and sister. Her ears stand right up now and she actually purrs. The other kittens don't. I don't know whether it's because they can't or don't want to. Like me. I can purr but usually I don't want to.

• • •

The Lions Gate Bridge still looms out of the misty grey when Aunt Mary and Uncle Robert come home in the late afternoon without Lizzie. Aunt Mary and I prepare supper side by side in the kitchen as she tells me every detail of her day.

"We got to the paediatric clinic right on time. Finding a place to park in the lot was the hardest part, it was so full. The clinic itself felt familiar — we've been there so often over the years. The doctor was running a few minutes late, so we sat. I must say your Uncle Rob fidgeted. I almost told him to go to the corner and play with the toys." Aunt Mary grins. But I can feel the anxiety behind her attempt at humour. I finish peeling the potatoes.

"Thanks, dear. Let's do some squash and carrots too. We can put them all together in the oven." She pushes the carrots towards me and begins hacking at the squash with a large knife. "When the door to the doctor's office finally opened, another girl came out with her parents. She looked younger than Lizzie and pretty frail. The nurse introduced her to us as Karen. She has the same heart problem as Lizzie and is going to be operated on tomorrow too."

"But I thought Lizzie said the girl who was to be operated on the same day was called Ingrid."

"You're right. That's what they told us last time." Aunt Mary's face clouds. "Afterwards, Lizzie asked the nurse about her. She said Ingrid died last week. Her face looked grey. I couldn't be a nurse. So much sadness." I'm sure my face is grey too. I wish I hadn't asked the question. Aunt Mary probably wishes I hadn't as well.

"The nurse tried to get the girls to talk. Your Uncle Rob and I shook hands with Karen's parents and mumbled something about seeing them on the ward. It was awkward — it's hard to know what to say. Apparently the girls won't be in the same room. They get private ones because the nurses and doctors need to watch them closely and they want them in contact with as few germs as possible."

"Will I get to see her? Lizzie, I mean." I chop the peeled carrots into large chunks and add them to the potato pile.

"I'm not sure. We'll try to arrange it, unofficially, even."

"Anyway, at this point the doctor called us in. He did the usual stuff and we asked the same old questions and found our way to the ward by lunch."

"What's the food like?"

"You and your stomach." Aunt Mary laughs at me. "Lizzie's tray didn't look bad, though — an egg sandwich, applesauce, milk, and a rolled-oat cookie — and we had to go down to the cafeteria."

"What's her room like?"

"There's a nice bright window overlooking the parking lot, a small locker for her clothes, and a bedside table. Lizzie put her three favourite books there: *The Secret Garden, Swallows and Amazons,* and, of course, *Anne of Green Gables.*" Aunt Mary daubs the squash pieces with butter and brown sugar and pops them in the oven. "What about you? Are they favourites of yours too?"

"I've never read *Swallows and Amazons.* But *The Secret Garden* and *Anne,* of course." I reach for the pile of potatoes and carrots. "Do we put these in the oven now too, Aunt Mary?"

"Not yet, dear. We'll wait until the squash cooks a little." She tosses oil and salt and pepper through the vegetables in the rectangular pan. "I told Lizzie she was not even to think about homework while she's in hospital. There will be lots of time later."

"And I can help her." My head whispers, *I sure hope so.* "What did the doctor say about the operation, about her chances?" I can see the shadow return to my aunt's face. Why does my tongue flap so easily? I didn't need to ask. I already know the answer. Maybe I just hope it'll be a different one this time.

"He said there's a fifty-fifty chance of the operation working. If it goes well, Lizzie will live to a ripe old age, grow up as a normal woman. Even marry and have children if she wants."

"And what happens if it doesn't go well?"

"Dr. Robertson said then they might do the operation again at a later date." My aunt's body suddenly looks small, her face more lined than I remembered. She removes a pan from the refrigerator. "I almost forgot to put the meat loaf in." The whoosh of hot dry air hits me as she opens the oven again.

Lines of fear and worry grip and crisscross my aunt's face. I think of how, for all these days and weeks and even the months after Mum died, I've been thinking only of me. Last month Aunt Mary reminded me that all the family was sad and unhappy about my mother. Now, I realize — how stupid could I have been — the same is happening with this operation. All what's in my head is probably in Aunt Mary's head, in Uncle Robert's head, in Dad's head. Even in Lizzie's grandmother's head.

At supper no one mentions Lizzie's empty chair.

• • •

I don't sleep much that night. When I finally do, I wake up shouting, "That's wrong. That's wrong. What have you done?" In my dream Lizzie had her leg cut off. She was lying in a pool of blood, her left leg off to the side but looking more like the leg of a deer on the side of the road. I lie awake for another hour, my brain troubled and confused.

In the morning, Aunt Mary and Uncle Robert look like they haven't slept well either, their faces are drawn and pale. They go off early, unsure of exactly when the surgery is to be because the other girl is first. I guess they just need to be with Lizzie. I wish I could be there too.

Instead, my body goes to school. My mind doesn't. *Please God, look after Lizzie.* I thought I didn't believe in God. *I promise to be better, not to be so mean. Or think bad thoughts.* I've been feeling sorry for me when I should be strong. Strong like Lizzie. Strong for Lizzie. *Please God. Please.*

• • •

On the way to HPD — much easier to say than Health and Personal Development — I dash into the washroom. There are two others waiting in line for the toilets. One is Dolores. She's in an old pleated skirt and a baggy sweater this time, no makeup. I try to make conversation.

"How are things?" Meaning of course, the running away.

"Fine." She's back to the can't-you-get-it-that-I-don't-want-to-talk mode.

"How's Stella? She's really nice."

"Fine." It's definitely can't-you-get-it-that-I-don't-want-to-talk. The four stalls all empty out together. Dolores and

I sit quietly as the others wash and leave.

I call to her. "Your eyes are a really pretty blue, Dolores. I never noticed them before." With the mascara, all I'd ever seen was the flipping lashes. There's a grunt from the other stall. "I'm serious. The casual look suits you." The pee-dribbling sound from next door stops. I hear the scuffle of toilet paper, clothes, the door open, and a very quick exit. Oh well.

• • •

After school I run next door to see Juniper again. This time Stella is there.

"Aren't they adorable? Their heads are so big and their tails stand up like little sticks." Not coming every day, she sees an even bigger change than I do.

"Are you going to get a kitten too?"

She snuggles one ball of fluff under her chin. "I don't think Dad will let us."

"How is Mrs. Taylor related to you?" I grab Juniper as she tumbles out of the cat bed.

"She's Dad's sister. But he doesn't like her very much. He says she's really bossy. Especially about us not going to church and all. But I like her. Do you like your Dad, Nora?"

"Oh sure. He's nice most of the time. I don't see him much because he's either away at work or in his room reading."

"Do you like your Mum?"

I don't stop to think. I just blurt it out. "She died last May."

"Oh. I'm sorry, Nora." A long silence. I pat the cats, cursing again my flapping tongue. "I guess having a mean parent is better than not having one at all."

She's a sweet kid.

• • •

To Nora,
> *Roses are red*
> *Violets are blue*
> *Sugar is sweet*
> *And so are you.*
>> *With love, Aunt Alice*

To my friend Nora,
> *What does the bee gather?*
> *That's right. Honey!*
> *And that's what Nora is,*
> *Just a honey, honey, honey.*
>> *Jeanie McQuaig*

Can I say the same for me?

16

The phone rings. I jump. Dad jumps.

"Hello. The Mackenzie house, Alan speaking." Pause. "Oh, Mrs. Quinn." My face falls. "Thanks. I'll send her over for it." The receiver clunks on the hook. "You left your umbrella at the Quinns'. She just noticed it."

It's about eight o'clock. We've been waiting and waiting. Uncle Robert and Aunt Mary have not come home from the hospital. Dad and I made a big batch of Spanish rice, thinking that would feed everyone, but it sits warming in the oven, half eaten.

"Why don't they phone?" I shuffle the pack of cards and begin another game of Patience. Doing homework is impossible.

"Oh, there are not many phones, and I am sure others are trying to use them too." Dad rattles the pages of the newspaper. I can tell he's trying to read. Or pretending.

"I'll go for the umbrella, Dad. I can't stand this sitting around any longer."

• • •

Mrs. Quinn opens the door. "How's Lizzie, dear?" She hands me the umbrella.

"We haven't heard yet."

"Poor lamb. I'm holding my breath too."

• • •

I run back home even though half of it is uphill. Again as I turn the corner at Moody Avenue there are shadows. This time, not on the ground, but on the low cement wall. "Hi Dolores. Hi Stella. Do you run away every night?" That's not the nicest of things to say, or the most sensitive. But as usual my mouth and tongue move long before my brain kicks in.

"Our dad gets drunk and does bad things to her." Stella cuddles up to her sister.

"Oh, shush Stella." Stella ducks the swat and pushes away.

"Lori, it's true. That's what you say. You say that's why we run away."

"Yeah, and he uses Mum as a punching bag when she's not at work. I don't know why Mum doesn't leave him." Dolores all but shouts at me, spitting it out like it's all my fault. Like I caused it. "And when she's not home he does dirty things to me."

The embarrassed silence seems to go on forever.

Finally I say, "Do you need some place to go?"

"We're fine."

"Are you warm enough?"

"I said we're fine." It's that I-don't-want-to-talk place again.

"Well. Okay. I gotta run because Lizzie had a big operation today and we haven't heard. But if you ever need somewhere to go you can always come to our place. See yah."

Why did I say that? About Lizzie. About staying at our place.

Maybe this is what Mrs. Quinn was talking about. Maybe I'm taking off my mask.

• • •

We wait and wait. I will Aunt Mary and Uncle Robert to phone. *Phone. Phone. Now.* But no telephone call. Dad checks his watch.

"Nora. It's ten-thirty. Long past bedtime. Go now, and straight to sleep. You have school tomorrow." My face contorts. I can feel it. "Yes, I know. You want to hear. But you'll hear in the morning. Losing sleep won't help them or Lizzie and it will definitely hurt you at school." I go to bed. But not to sleep.

• • •

Much later I hear voices. I may have drifted off because I didn't hear the door open or them come up the stairs. I hear their hushed tones and tip-toe to the door. Something tells me not to run wildly into the living room.

"Oh, Alan." It's Aunt Mary. "It was so hard. I know we should have phoned. But we wanted good news. And when the nurse asked them to move to another room and said she died...."

I take a deep breath and fly back to bed. *Lizzie dead. Lizzie dead. Lizzie dead.*

How can it be? *Mum, oh Mum.*

Not another one.

Lizzie dead.

I can't stand it.

What will I do with the Autograph book I bought Lizzie for Christmas?

What a stupid thing to think.

Lizzie dead. Lizzie dead. Lizzie dead.

Oh Mum, oh Mum, oh Mum.

• • •

> *To my dearest friend and cousin,*
> *Away in a forest*
> *Carved on a tree*
> *Are two little words,*
> *"Remember Me."*
>
> > *Love, Lizzie*

17

The house is pitch-dark when I crawl out of bed. I pull on my warmest clothes — wool skirt, long socks, heavy sweater. I creep into the kitchen, pour myself cornflakes and milk. The fridge hums in the silence. I take several bananas and an apple from the fruit bowl for lunch. I don't want to wake the others. Or face them. At least not yet.

It's 7:00 a.m. The early November morning greyness drifts over the mountains as I unlatch the back door. I slip into my coat and wrap a scarf around my neck. The usual heavy clouds are gone. What remain are far-up strands of wispy cirrus, chasing rapidly across the sky. The damp air nips my face. I dig into my pockets for mittens. The unpleasantness of the day barely registers.

Mum, wherever you are, look after Lizzie. My heavy legs stumble up the street. *Why wasn't it me? Then I could be with you, Mum.*

I kick at a stray pile of leaves. The few dry ones lift and fly, the wet ones underneath fall back with a soggy plop. I see Lizzie's face, I remember her words. "It's my one chance for a big life." She made her choice, even though she knew it might not work. She was so brave. She was so brave. If only I could be like her.

Fists in my pocket, school bag drooping off my right shoulder, I walk and walk. Skulk up back alleys, turn corner after corner, head down.

• • •

"Hiya, Nora. You look sad." It's Stella, holding Dolores's hand. "What's wrong?"

"Nothing." I wipe my face with my sleeve. "What are you doing here?"

"Lori always walks with me to school."

"Want to come with us?" It's Dolores this time.

"Sure. Where to?" It will help me not to think.

"To Ridgeway Elementary." I kick another clump of leaves. Stella does too.

"You know last night, when I said you could come over? I mean it. If it ever happens again, come to our house. Just come. Even if it's late in the night. Both of you."

"Really? You're sure?" Dolores's face brightens. She's wearing the same old skirt and baggy sweater under a half-open rain coat. No mascara and eyeliner again. "Your family won't mind?"

"Of course not." I'd better warn Dad.

There are kids already at the school. A group of girls playing jacks on the front steps, another jumping hopscotch into half-faded chalk marks on the sidewalk. Boys roll marbles. Other girls skip. A rope thwacks the pavement. Feet clomp.

I'm a little Dutch girl dressed in blue
Here are the things that I can do —
Salute to the captain, bow to the queen
Turn myself around like a washing machine.
I can do a tap dance, I can do the splits
I can do the hokey-pokey just like this.

The chanting of the girls pounds in my head. Salute
to the captain, bow to the queen. Bow to the queen.
Like old times, me skipping, Lizzie turning rope.

• • •

The day grinds by, with my mind and heart not present.
I didn't tell Dolores about Lizzie and fortunately she
didn't ask.

Yesterday, school was bad. Today, it's worse than bad.
In front of the class Mrs. Bramley asks me why I missed
rehearsal yesterday. I feel my face redden. "I forgot," is
all I say. Which is completely true. Then she carries on
with a long sermon about the commitment and hard
work needed by everybody — in other words, me — if
we're going to get this musical into top shape. Of course
I disappear into the floor. I hate being singled out in class.

In PT we run around the track again. My legs are
still heavy. They feel like stumps of wood barely connected to my body. Mrs. Grantham yells from the
sidelines, "Come on, Nora, where's your oomph? You
can do better than that." And in Math, Mr. Keen, who
never ever has anyone go to the board, sends me up first
thing and each answer I get wrong. He makes me stay

in at noon to finish my homework. I guess he figures I've been slacking. I get madder and madder as the day goes on. Mad at myself for coming to school and mad at everyone else for being mean.

I can't do PT. I can't do Math. I don't want to be at school but I don't want to go home. I don't want to go home to more death.

• • •

Instead, I run next door for a pat of Juniper and Carmody. The warmth of their little bodies is comforting. Juniper's purr on my chest resonates down my body, like when I sing. I ask Mrs. Taylor about why Dolores never comes over.

"I like Stella here, but Dolores is a bad influence." Her mouth pinches. "Her makeup and tight clothes tell me all I want to know about Dolores. The less Stella is around her the better."

"Dolores doesn't wear makeup or tight clothes any-more." Mrs. Taylor flicks a pillowcase out straight, then folds it in thirds, and thirds again. "I haven't seen her with a cigarette either."

"Well, I'm glad to hear that. Maybe she's finally getting some sense."

"Oh, I don't think it's about sense. It's something about trying to be a different person." I don't know why I know that, but I do. I feel it. "Sometimes I see them huddling outside on the street. Stella says they're running away from home, that their dad does bad and dirty things to Dolores."

Mrs. Taylor's face flinches, turns red, then white. "What did you say?" She stoops to pick up a dropped tea towel. "What did you say?" she repeats. Then I remember. Their dad is Mrs. Taylor's brother.

"Stella told me that when her father drinks he does awful things to Dolores. I think Dolores is worried he's going to do that to Stella too." I'm surprised at the words coming out of my mouth. I'd not thought about it before. But I'm happy I said it. Mrs. Quinn's mask again. We shouldn't wear masks. If Mrs. Taylor doesn't like it — or Dolores — too bad. "I told them they can come to our house anytime they need to — to get away from him."

The more I talk, the more Mrs. Taylor looks like someone — I guess that's me — has hit her in the stomach. Her hands fumble with the remaining tea towels. At last she sits down, almost like her muscles are so drained she can't stand up any longer. "I don't know what the bad and dirty things are, but that's what they said."

I continue stroking the kittens. They crawl up my arm to my shoulder. Mrs. Taylor sits and sits. I wonder what I've done. Have I done something bad myself? But I don't think so.

At last she says, "Thank-you, Nora. Thank you for telling me." Her voice sounds as drained as her face looks.

"Are you okay, Mrs. Taylor?"

"I'll be fine. You run along home now."

• • •

The house is empty and cold. Where are Aunt Mary and Uncle Robert? Why would Dad go to the hospital on a day like today? And there's no note.

It's useless to do homework. Anyway, I don't plan on going to school tomorrow. I pull the ironing board out of the wall and attack the clean laundry in the basket. I iron pillowcases, tea towels, shirts, and blouses. I iron the underpants, which normally I ignore, even though my mum used to iron them. I put on my favourite record, *Windjammer*. It's all cheerful and upbeat. I can't or won't put on something sad.

Like when her mother, my Grandma Gladwin, died. Mum had come home from up north — Bella Coola, I think it was — to nurse her, and the rest of the family was away at church when she died. Mum went straight to her bedroom and put on her most cheerful dress, one with tiny yellow flowers all over, one she knew her mother loved. That's how she greeted the rest of the family when they came back. She knew her mother wouldn't want black.

And neither would Lizzie. Lizzie would want cheerfulness and happy music.

As I iron, I sing out the jaunty tunes at the top of my voice: "Life on the ocean waves where friendships ..." Tears well up. "And while we sail the waves, I wave my love goodbye; the kisses that she saves, I'll gather by and by." But the words make my tears flow, as the ironed clothes pile up, as the smell of hot steamy cotton invades my senses.

At 5:30, I put the contents of two large containers of spaghetti sauce from the freezer on to heat, and fill a big pot of water. When Mum died, I remember how friends and neighbours dropped by. Even if I didn't like the baked beans or gloppy casserole they brought, it was good to have them. Both the people and the food. Here there's no one. No church members. No neighbours who know us or know Lizzie.

Then I have a thought — maybe Dad's gone to bring Dorothy and Jan home. Something in me feels better. I want people around now. I peel apples for apple crisp. Every curl of the peel reminds me of Lizzie. We used to try to do the whole apple in one kinky curly curl. Like her hair.

I place the arm at the beginning of the *Windjammer* record for the third time. The music blasts forth again. The front door opens. Despite the noise from the player, I jump.

"Oh, Aunt Mary." I fly into my aunt's arms and burst into tears. "I'm so sorry. I'm so sorry." Aunt Mary gives me a squeeze and then holds me away from her body with her arms straight. Her face is normal, normal tired, but not scrunched up and miserable looking.

"Honey, honey. What have you done that you're so sorry for?"

"For Lizzie, for ..." I can't say the word.

"For what?" Aunt Mary brushes away the mussy hair on my tear-stained cheeks. "Lizzie's doing great. What on earth made you think otherwise? Didn't you see the message on your blackboard? Why do you think there's a smile on my face?"

"But, but, last night. When you came in you said she died. I heard you." I crumple to the stair, shaking. "Are you sure she's all right? You're not pretending?"

She nods. Her face queries Uncle Robert at the door behind her.

"Oh, my darling child. We would never pretend about something like that." My uncle sweeps me up in his arms and carries me to the living room couch. "Here. Now let's explain what has happened, every little detail in the past twenty-four hours. Then maybe you'll believe us." Aunt Mary turns down the record player. The music dances on. "But let me say first that the doctor is happy with the operation so far, and Lizzie seems to be breathing well and strongly. She even opened her eyes and said a very weak hello."

They tell me of their day and the day before too. Mainly of their wait.

"The other girl, Karen, went for surgery first. When we got there we had to wait in the hall because Lizzie was undergoing all the preparatory work. But we had lots of time to talk in her room when they had finished and that was good. We even got to walk her down the hall towards the surgery. But the hard part was watching her go through those doors without us." Uncle Robert pauses and wipes his eyes. "Being a parent, you want to protect your child from all hurts. And we couldn't." His voice is gravelly.

"Then we had to wait and wait. That was even worse. We were taken to a room for family members. The parents of Karen were there too. We all waited but no one talked much. A whisper here. A whisper there." I'm in the middle of the chesterfield between my aunt and uncle. At first one speaks, then the other. I notice grey in Aunt Mary's hair in just the same place Mum had it.

"Eventually I went down to the cafeteria. Your aunt couldn't leave. Or wouldn't. We really didn't feel like eating, but nibbling on the sandwiches I brought back gave us something to do."

"About then a nurse came in and asked Karen's parents to come with her. Marlene, the mother, started to cry, 'What's wrong? What's wrong?' Her face was white as the proverbial sheet. She began to wail — a wail that came from somewhere deep within, but sounded more like it was from something unearthly." Aunt Mary enfolds me in a rocking hug.

"I must admit I felt huge relief it wasn't Lizzie. Then I felt terrible. That poor mother. Later, when the nurse came back, I asked, 'Is she going to die?' I meant Karen, of course. She shook her head back and forth but you could tell she was putting her best face on." Funny how when you're upset, you notice things that don't really matter. Like all I can see is the deep shadow on Uncle Robert's jaw and think, *he should shave.*

"At this point Lizzie was still in surgery. I guess the nurse couldn't say much. And besides, she didn't want to upset us. She said only that Karen's parents were talking with the other doctors. That's all."

It's like a roller coaster ride at the Penticton Peach Festival. Up and down, up and down, with my stomach left in the air, wondering if it'll ever land. Too much.

"So we waited and waited. We waited to hear about Lizzie. But we also waited to hear about the other girl. I think that's what you heard. You heard me telling your dad." Aunt Mary squeezes me again. "Little Karen died last night. She got through the surgery but something happened after. Our Lizzie is fine. We even got to see her. That's why we were so late. They let us into the Recovery Room for just one minute. We had to gown up. She was sleeping."

Without a sob of warning, Aunt Mary bursts into tears. It's like the dam holding back days and months and even years of tears broke. I cry with her. I thought in the last few months I had spilled every last tear possible. Yet there's more. And now I'm not sure who these tears are for. For Mum? For Aunt Mary and Uncle Robert? For Lizzie? For me? But this batch seems to soften my insides at last.

"We've been at the hospital all day. You don't know how good it was to see her." Uncle Robert blows into a handkerchief; then shoves it back into his side pocket. "The doctor said she isn't out of the woods yet."

I raise my arm to wipe my face on my sleeve, but Aunt Mary, with her own hankie soggy with tears, daubs the wet from my cheeks. Her gentle strokes comfort. Funny, I don't even mind the crumpled feeling. It's like the crumply me is now waiting to be filled up with laughter and hope and warmth and tomorrows.

Curtains drawn back, the sun struggles to brighten Lizzie's room. A pot of flowers adds a smiling warmth to the institutional plainness.

"Elizabeth, my dear, I have a surprise for you this morning." Aunt Mary has on her whispery voice. Lizzie opens her eyes to a narrow slit. "Your dad went back to Penticton to see to the boys, remember, so I brought someone else instead."

I stare at my cousin, my best friend. She looks entirely different. But how can that be? A nurse in a starchy white uniform with a small bunchy cap hurries in. I see what Dorothy will be like in a few years. "Shall we show them, Lizzie?" Her voice booms. Lizzie winces and opens her eyes fully. She smiles at me and nods.

The nurse fusses down at the bottom of the bed. Lizzie unbends her legs and wiggles her feet down to where the bedclothes are rolled back. Her feet peek out. For all the world to see. First ten toes, then her arches, her heels. And they are all pink. Her pale, pale skin that always had a purple or blue tinge, is now all pink. That's what's different.

I begin to cry. *Not again*, I think.

Then I laugh as I realize these tears are tears of joy.

• • •

Lizzie will have to be in the hospital at least three weeks, the doctors say. Aunt Mary continues to visit her every day. And almost every night we phone Uncle Robert in Penticton. I talk to him and Dougie and Jack before I pass the phone to Aunt Mary. Long distance is really expensive, but Dad doesn't seem to mind the cost. I guess it's about family — they are the closest family we have.

Aunt Mary takes charge of the house. She does most of the cooking and laundry. I help but I don't have to organize it, remind Dad to buy the food, or change his bedclothes. I don't know if it's because Aunt Mary's around, but Dad talks a lot about Mum. At first it's awkward. Then it becomes more natural. A *remember when* sends us off telling some story of our lives together. Even pictures of Mum now reappear on the piano and the living room side table.

• • •

I still have twice weekly practices of *The Wizard of Oz* after school. I know all the pieces now and, where there's harmony, even have my alto part memorized. Sometimes I sit with Jonathon — he has gorgeous eyes and a really cute smile — but mostly with Ava and Alvina. I volunteer at noon on Wednesdays for costumes. A girl in grade nine is organizing it with Miss Croft, the new, young Home Ec teacher. She's doing the sewing half of our course in January and we get to make a dress.

Many evenings Aunt Mary and even Jan, when she's home, play the piano for a sing-a-long. I find I can hear the inner harmonies, so reading the alto line is easy. Jan says that's a talent. Sunday nights Dad lets me curl up with Aunt Mary and watch *The Ed Sullivan Show*.

Friday I go to Ava and Alvina's place after school. They have a rambling old house that needs a coat of paint. It was their grandparents', and everywhere on the walls are oils by their grandfather, including a painting of a set of baby twins.

"Yeah, that's us," says Alvina. "Grandpa died not long after he finished it." At school the girls don't talk much; they stick out only because of their twoness. At home they talk and laugh a mile a minute.

"He did that one," Ava points to a watercolour on the other wall, "when he was not much older than we are now. We want to be able to paint like him."

Their bedroom upstairs is bright and happy. Watercolour paintings of flowers and trees and people cover the pale yellow walls. Even paintings of the dark, dank coastal forest have a life about them. "Wow. You guys are good." I like their quiet enthusiasm, their love of the outdoors. I want to be their friend.

Later that night, Dolores and Stella come over. It's snowing big sloppy flakes. They have only slacks and long-sleeved cardigans on. Stella's bottom lip quivers. I assume she's been crying. But I don't comment. I know what it's like when you don't want to tell others about your tears. Aunt Mary insists they eat some of the leftover squash soup we had for supper. Even though they said *no* to it at first, they end up eating two bowlfuls each.

While I do homework, they watch TV. When Aunt Mary asks them to sleep over, Dolores says it's time to go. We walk them home and wait until they flick on and off the front light to show they're okay.

But are they okay?

The next morning, Aunt Mary and I meet Dot and Janet in downtown Vancouver for a birthday shopping spree. Dad gave them strict instructions to get me new school clothes and an outfit for good, including shoes. We choose a green flared skirt with a beautiful crinoline — scratchy, but what crinoline isn't — a pair of pumps for special occasions and a pair of penny loafers for school, a twin sweater set, and a matching brown-flecked wool skirt. It must have cost a fortune, but who am I to complain?

"You can come with me to church tomorrow in your new outfit," says Aunt Mary. That's not exactly what I had in mind but going anywhere with my aunt is more than okay. More like wonderful. Even church. And besides, I might have changed my opinion about God now.

And last but not least, Aunt Mary says, "Let's fit you with your first bra." I am sure I turn red from the top of my head to the tips of my toes, almost as red and embarrassed as last Tuesday when I had to call Aunt Mary because I got my first period.

• • •

The next day, Sunday, is my actual birthday. Jan and Dorothy — would you believe Dot? — make my favourite meal, lasagna and salad. Aunt Mary had baked a cake and hidden it in the freezer in the basement. We eat most of it, including lashings of thick chocolate icing, but I save some for Lizzie.

That evening I lie on the old carpet of the screened-in porch next door, twitching a piece of wool at Juniper. When Mrs. Taylor appears, I say in a casual sort of voice, "Dolores and Stella came to our house Friday night. They were cold and Stella was crying."

"Who else saw them?" Mrs. Taylor's face has a funny hard look.

"Dad and Aunt Mary of course. Why?" She doesn't answer. "We gave them some leftover soup. Later, we walked them home." Mrs. Taylor doesn't say much but that funny hard look around her mouth becomes more pinched in.

• • •

Room 709
Vancouver General Hospital
November 22, 1959
Delivered by Shank's Mare (that is, Mum)

Dear Nora,
I know it seems silly to write when you're just across the water in North Van, but this gives me something else to do besides reading when Mum's not here. So where to begin? At the beginning, I guess.

The first things I remember are the high bed, the hard mattress, crawling under the covers with the tightly pulled sheets that smelled like soap and, well, that it was all like that before. That's what I noticed first. It was being in a hospital again. Sort of obvious, because I was. But it also brought back the loneliness. Even the sheets smelled like loneliness. You probably think that's crazy, but they do. They don't smell and feel comforting like fresh sheets at home.

When Mum and Dad left the first day it was the worst. Worse than when they were here and worse than before. I strained to hear the sound of their feet as they walked away. But they blended in with voices, telephones ringing, and other footsteps. I felt my heart beating right up in my throat. I tried reading *The Secret Garden.* I couldn't concentrate. I tried *Anne.* My mind went nowhere in particular. I peered out the window to the hospital wing opposite, wondering who was there and why and for how long.

I was scared. I didn't tell Mum. That fifty-fifty chance the next day kept blinking in my head. Particularly, the fifty percent chance of not working. But I kept saying the alternative was a hundred to zero, the zero part not being much of an alternative. When I thought about it that way I felt better.

That night I slept like a log because they gave me a sleeping pill. The next morning I couldn't have any food, only water, so my stomach growled all morning. One not-so-nice part was that the nurse shaved the hair between my legs. That was completely awful, embarrassing, and a whole bunch of other words. Now my incision goes from the top to the bottom of my front. Funny, though, there were so many nurses and doctors poking and prodding my body and talking and pushing stethoscopes at me I pretty much ended up forgetting to be shy.

Other than that Mum and Dad came, most of the morning was a blur until I crawled onto the gurney. That's the thin bed on wheels they take you on for an operation. Those sheets smelled different. Not of loneliness, more of fear, or of the unknown. Weird how smells can make me think of emotions. I wonder how many kids have gone on that gurney under those sheets for operations like mine and not like mine.

Mum and Dad walked with me to the surgery doors. Their faces were upside down, their mouths sort of falling to meet their noses and their eyes puffed out. Oh, Nora, my dad who laughs at the antics of Jack and Dougie, who prunes his fruit trees and digs in the garden, picks the peaches with the same sort of loving eyes he uses for Mum and even us, the dad who plays ball with all the boys of the neighbourhood as I keep score, that man who goes to church every Sunday, that's the dad I've known. But he squeezed my hand and tears rolled silently down his face the whole time. I didn't know that person. It made me more scared because he wasn't him.

Mum was different too. You know, she doesn't usually talk a whole lot. Sometimes, but not most of the time. This time she babbled on, telling me you sent hugs and good luck and stuff like that. Words flew past me — over my head. It was like they were heading for the dust motes that hung in the sunlight as we passed each open doorway. She also gave me tight, tight hugs. Maybe you've noticed, she's been giving hugs lately. I'm not sure why. I sort of liked it and still do, but it definitely is different, especially the tight kind. The beige ceiling with the occasional crack slid by.

I remember Mum's squeeze, felt Dad's kiss on my forehead, their upside down faces.

I remember scrunching their hands back and saying, "Bye, Mum. Bye, Dad. See you in a while." And Mum's last words, "Remember our deal," and me nodding.

The next thing I saw was scorpions crawling all over everything. Scorpions in a hospital? I've never seen scorpions but that's what it looked like. Big spiders seemed to be crawling all over the world. I held my breath. I was so afraid. I remember thinking a scream might dislodge them, send them careening down on top of me. Another part of me wanted to scream out anyway and knock them down, but the bed clothes were pulled tightly over me, my arms pinned underneath. Then I decided I was sleeping and it was a nightmare. Even thinking about it now brings back a bit of that fear.

A nurse rushed in. Maybe I did scream. But all she said was, "Oh, you're awake. Wonderful. How do you feel, Elizabeth?" She peered in as if behind glass. She was covered with scorpions too. I closed my eyes. I breathed in. The air smelled funny. I relaxed. I remembered what the doctor said, that after the operation I would be in a plastic tent, a tent with a funny sweet smell, giving me extra oxygen to help me breathe. I felt stupid. I remember thinking, though, why if my heart was fixed would I need help to breathe? I never asked.

The first time I saw Mum and Dad, that really was when I knew my nightmare or dream was over. I wanted to hug them but they were behind the tent too. And covered with scorpions of course. Eventually, I realized the scorpions were spots of rust or something on the plastic.

Mostly I remember being oh-so tired and that seemed to go on for days.

This is a hugely long letter and I'll run out of paper soon. Two more big items. My most embarrassing moment — I had my first period, lying here in bed. There was a slimy wet feeling between my legs. I tried to sit up and the next thing there was blood all over the sheets. I pulled the cord for the nurse. And my saddest moment — Karen's parents came in to see me, bringing a pot of flowers. I don't know what kind they are but they are pretty. I felt horrible. After they left I cried and cried. I was the lucky fifty percent. I'm glad for me, I'm glad for Mum and Dad. But so so sad for Karen and her parents.

Anyway, that's the end of the page. I won't start another. I'll see you at your house next week, they say. Hugs to my favourite cousin.

Lizzie

PS Happy (belated) Birthday. Did Mum give you the present I brought down for you?

Lizzie comes home three weeks to the day — November 29 — after her operation. The Sunday before, I put up a welcome home sign for her, of course. I make my bed up fresh and put the other mattress on the floor for me. I clear the desk of all my books so she has a place to study and bring up an old table from the basement for me to work on. Aunt Mary hangs Lizzie's clothes in my closet and I stuff my underwear, socks, and pyjamas into two drawers so Lizzie can have the two other drawers of my bureau. It's a squeeze but should be fun.

I wait until now to ask Dad if we can have Juniper. A little late because I wasn't sure he'd let me. I have lots of arguments figured out in my head — like I work so hard in the house I deserve to have something I want; like I babysit and save my own money; like cats are good mousers and we don't want mice in our basement; like Mrs. Taylor needs a home for her; and the clincher, I figure, Lizzie will have company when she moves home. And lo and behold without me saying any of that he says, "Great idea."

When I tell him Mrs. Taylor says we can have her on Tuesday, Dad says, "I'll get some canned food on my way home tomorrow." It bowls me over.

The kitten will live in a basket in Lizzie's and my bedroom. She's still young — Juniper, I mean. I cross my fingers she won't cry for her mother.

Like me.

• • •

Aunt Mary takes the bus back to Penticton a few days after Lizzie gets settled in here. I take over more of the running of the house, but she has put loads of cooked meals in the freezer for us. Lizzie and I do homework together every day and play with each other's hair most nights. Hers is growing longer. From time to time I put it up in a curly ponytail but it looks better down. Of course she does mine in a French braid, sometimes even before school. As she gets stronger, she makes muffins or cookies during the day and helps me with meals when I get home. And plays with Juniper, of course.

Dolores and Stella drop by a lot, once more at night, but mostly together on their way to or from the Taylors' and the kittens. They say they're coming to see Juniper but, if you ask me, I think they like it here. Dolores is not so snippy any more, even at school. The day before yesterday, Stella asked if I would come over some time to her place. I really didn't want to, because of what Trudy said before, so I told Lizzie about it. We decided we'd go together.

Their mother works at Safeway, and the house is pretty ratty and run down. It smells stale. Stella says their dad has left them. Apparently their aunt and uncle — the Taylors, next door, of course — told him to go and never come back. And he did. I guess that's why the girls are both over at the Taylors' more. Anyway, it's Stella's birthday next week, on December the seventeenth. Dolores invited us for a surprise party and a sleepover. I think she has invited another little girl and maybe Trudy. Dad says we can go to the party but, because of Lizzie's health, not the sleepover. We told Dolores we would make the birthday cake, so Stella won't see it. It's been a long time since I've been to a party.

• • •

Two days later, when I come home from school, Lizzie has written on my chalkboard.

> **The hole in my heart is almost better. How about yours?**

What do I say? Instead I hand her the Autograph book I was going to give her at Christmas. I write on the first page:

> *Dear Lizzie (my favourite cousin and best friend),*
>   *First in your Album*
>   *First in your thoughts*
>   *First to be remembered—*
>   *Last to be forgot.*
>   *Love and hugs, Nora*

• • •

"Dad?" My dad's kneeling in the snow-spotted vegetable garden pulling the last of the carrots. He has turned leaves into the rest of the soil, leaving the parsnips to sweeten over the winter. "Dad," I say again. He seems off in the distance, away with the fairies as my grandmother says.

"Hmmm? What is it dear?" He pauses in his pulling.

"I want to take piano lessons from Betsy Betuzzi." I rush on before he can interrupt. "I advertised at the library and two teachers answered. One lives in Lynn Valley. That's too far away. But Betsy Betuzzi lives on 16th Street. I went to see her. I like her."

"Whoa, girl. What's all this about?"

"Remember I said I wanted piano lessons? And you said, 'We'll see.' Well I figured unless I did something about it, *we'll see* meant *no*. So I advertised. She's not much older than Dot." I race on, afraid Dad will stop me or won't listen. "She's been playing piano since she was little and has taught for three years from her parents' house. She lives on 16th. Oh, I already said that. That's close to school so I can take lessons on my way home."

Dad sits back on his heels, slaps his muddy garden gloves together, a thoughtful expression on his face. "If you really want to, of course you can take lessons from this Betsy person. But I have another idea for you." My beginning smile fades. I can feel me crumple up waiting for the worst. I pull my stocking cap further down over my ears and shiver.

"But —"

"Now, hold on. Just hear me out." He sighs, pushes himself up and grabs the bucket of carrots. "Let's go in. I'm getting cold." We climb the stairs. "Ten days ago I received a letter from my old clinic in Penticton. They still haven't found anyone to replace me." I breathe in. I can guess what's coming. "They want me back. My residency here is going fine. I do like it. But I've been mulling their offer over since the day it came. I talked to Jan and Dorothy." As I open the kitchen door and kick off my muddy shoes, I take an even deeper breath. A part of me gets angry. Yet again, he talks to my sisters before me. "They are okay with it. So we can go back to Penticton, if you really want to. And you can take piano lessons there, of course."

My head whirls. The wind catches the door. It slams behind us. I have exactly what I've been longing for, wanting desperately, for months. And despite my anger at Dad — maybe frustration is a better word — I know my answer immediately.

"You can take your time to think about it," he says.

I shake my head and smile. I don't have to think about it or even weigh the sides. How can I not know? "Thanks for asking, Dad. I'd love to move back to Penticton. Let's do it." I pause for the drama of it. I can see his face fall, his body sink. "But only after you finish your surgery training. Right now it's important that all of us, Jan and Dorothy, you and me, are together." I pause again, search for a smile on his face. "But thanks for thinking of me."

My dad has that queer look again, like he doesn't know who I am. "Are you sure?"

I nod. His face crumples. Tears well up in his eyes. "It's okay to cry, you know, Dad."

Acknowledgments

First and most importantly I wish to thank Bette Cannings, who was the inspiration for a part of this story and who let me use examples from her Autograph book. Thanks also to Dr. Neil Guenther, who generously reviewed the medical details for accuracy.

Various people read drafts of this manuscript: Bette Cannings, Linda Holman, Pat Boyd, and Rick Gray. Michelle Turner gave me invaluable editorial suggestions and Lorna Klohn helped me with historical details. They all have my gratitude.

Thanks also to Dundurn, specifically Sylvia McConnell, for believing in me.

By the same author

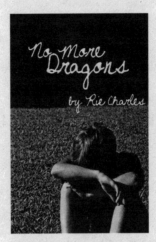

No More Dragons
by Rie Charles
9781926607122
$9.95

How do you turn an upside-down life right-side up? Thirteen-year-old Alex is afraid. Afraid of his dad, afraid of kids at school, worried about his sick brother and, most of all, angry at himself for being a wuss. How can he make his life different, become a new person that people like?

"I'm writing because its starting to get to me. Plus I need to tell someone," begins Alex. Through letters to his only friend, Alex breaks his solitude and confronts the truth.

As courage and wisdom gradually build, he gains the confidence to confront his own dragons.

Available at your favourite bookseller

 DUNDURN

Visit us at

Dundurn.com
@dundurnpress
Facebook.com/dundurnpress
Pinterest.com/dundurnpress